NORTH BRISTOL WRITERS

IN ASSOCIATION WITH IANDE PRESS

FIRE

Edited By

Pete W. Sutton

Chrissey Harrison

Barry Hollow

NORTH BRISTOL WRITERS

First published in 2021
by North Bristol Writers
in association with Iande Press.
www.northbristolwriters.wordpress.com

Edited by Pete W. Sutton, Chrissey Harrison & Barry Hollow.

Cover design and typeset by Chrissey Harrison.

A CIP catalogue record of this book is available
from the British Library.

ISBN 978-0-9554182-6-6
ebook available – ISBN 978-0-9554182-7-3

Printed and bound in the UK by IngramSpark.

Contents

Introduction   1
CHRISSEY HARRISON

I Am The Fire   5
BARRY HOLLOW

Born to Burn   9
CLARE DORNAN

Esau's Gift   15
CHLOE HEADDON

On the Run   40
CHRISSEY HARRISON

Up in Smoke   41
PETE W. SUTTON

Heated Words   49
KEN SHINN

The Crucible 66
BARRY HOLLOW

Sin Night 69
M. E. RODMAN

Evenfall 86
KEVLIN HENNEY

The Sancti 89
DEV AGARWAL

The Heat of the Forge 113
SCOTT LEWIS

Last Game 120
CLARE DORNAN

Long Hot Summer 121
NICK WALTERS

We Are Where We Are 139
KEVIN MACCABE

Four Poems 143
KIMBERLY NUGENT

The Comfort of Public
Fireplaces 149
B. ANNE ADRIAENS

Smoke 155
PETE W. SUTTON

Memories to the Flames   159
PETE W. SUTTON

Trace   177
AMANDA STAPLES

Tell Me Beautiful Lies   179
CHRISSEY HARRISON

Burning Desire   189
AMANDA STAPLES

Patience   192
BARRY HOLLOW

Brand   195
ALEX NICHOLAS

The Devil's Handmaidens   205
MARIA HERRING

Thirty Four Matches on the
Rising Scale of Happiness   224
CLARE DORNAN

About the Authors   227

Introduction

CHRISSEY HARRISON

Fire holds a unique place in the human psyche, deeply intertwining fear and fascination. From the entrancing flicker of a candle flame to the raw, elemental fury of a forest fire, Fire gives and takes away. We speak of it as alive and sentient – a fire can roar, leap, spit, even die. We even talk to it sometimes, feed and care for it like a child, until we think we understand it. But while we may bend it to our will for a time, such an abstract and unknowable force can never be entirely tamed.

Given this varied and complicated relationship, it comes as no surprise that choosing this theme for our fourth anthology yielded a varied and complicated collection of stories and poetry.

We see the human connection to Fire in *The Comfort of Public Fireplaces* (B. Anne Adriaens), *The Heat of the Forge* (Scott Lewis), and Clare Dornan's three pieces – *Born to Burn*, *Last Game* and *34 Matches on the Rising Scale of Happiness*. Drawing closer to the flames, we dabble with the seductive but sinister lure of Fire in *Long Hot Summer* (Nick Walters), *Smoke* (Pete W. Sutton), and *Tell Me Beautiful Lies* (Chrissey Harrison).

In *Burning Desire* and *The Devil's Handmaidens*, Amanda Staples and Maria Herring take us back to that dark chapter of Fire's history, the witch trials of the 17th Century. Meanwhile, Kevlin Henney and Dev Agarwal show us speculative futures where Fire is still brutal and inevitable in *Evenfall* and *The Sancti*. In our fantasy contributions – *Esau's Gift* (Chloe Headdon), *Brand* (Alex Nicholas), *Sin Night* (M. E. Rodman) and *Memories to the Flames* (Pete W. Sutton) – the authors put the power of Fire in markedly different hands with different motives.

Fire becomes an agent of chaos, a catalyst for good or ill, in *Up In Smoke* (Pete W. Sutton), *Trace* (Amanda Staples) and *On the Run* (Chrissey Harrison). Barry Hollow and Kimberly Nugent explore the lexicon and texture of Fire in their poetry. And rounding things out, Ken Shinn and Kevin MacCabe bring a little dark and allegorical humour to the mix with *Heated Words* and *We Are Where We Are*.

This anthology grew from the spark of North Bristol Writers' 2019 *Bristol Festival of Literature* event of the same name, where some of the stories were performed. As with our previous volumes, there are new and familiar faces; all talented authors at different stages in their writing journeys (which you can read more about in the About the Authors section at the end).

In the absence of an acknowledgement section (as is becoming a tradition), I want to thank my co-editors – Pete for reviewing and selecting the stories and the mammoth task of copy editing and Barry for curating the poetry and offering guidance on that front – and also Ian Millsted for editorial and publishing support, and all the contributors who peer critiqued and studiously polished their work.

Our theme is Fire, but in these stories, as in life, Fire is never just part of the background. It drives change and conflict by its very presence, a character more than a motif or a theme, and so we begin with an introduction by Barry Hollow to not *what*, but *who* is Fire.

Happy reading.

I Am The Fire

By Barry Hollow

I am the flames

I am the Sun

I am the day

I am the burn

I am the light

I show the way

I am the spirit

to lead you astray

I am the match

I am the fuse

I am the pyro-

maniacs muse

I am the brazier,

molten at core

I am the lion

Rampant to roar!

I am the pit
I am all hell
I am the flames
too wild to quell
I am the bomb
I am the blaze
I am the bonfire
watch me amaze!
I am the anger
I am the sin
I am the rage
I torch your kin
I am majestic
I am the heat
I am death knell
and force the retreat
I burn the bridge
I am infernal
I am the greed
and savage inferno
I am the kernel
I am the spark
I am the pilot
I kill the dark
I am the fever

I am the torch

I am the wrath

your earth will be scorched!

I am the spear tip,

hardened and cruel

I am the whoosh!

unleashed by your fuel

I eat the air

I burn to dust

I smoke the earth

as I raze to the crust

I breathe new life

I am the candle

I am the passion

Am I too hot to handle?

I warm to enchant

And I am the smoulder,

So smoulder with me

Near me

In me

On me

By me

Try me

I am fire!

Distant water cannot quench a fire nearby.

Born to Burn

By Clare Dornan

November 2016
Rwenzori Mountains, Uganda

For a moment I think of the chameleons, so tiny they straddled my finger. Miniature eyes, swivelling for flies. I should have searched for them, stuffed the pockets of my rucksack with them. My research notes, my pens, I grabbed fumbling. Sleeping bag, water bottle, head torch, quick Miss Kate, it's getting closer. Laptop, socks, fleece-used-as-a-pillow, diary, it's all with me.

But the tiny dwarf chameleons. The feathery moss that catches the morning dew. The bromeliads, the twisted trees of heather and scarlet-tufted sunbirds that would flit in the sunlight. I travelled so far to be with you. And now the roar thunders like a jet engine and you no longer exist, you sacred rare beauty.

Solomon's in front of me, his blade hacks the ferns and they scatter clean. We didn't come this way, where are we going? To the river, he says and my head is down, vines criss-cross like trip-wire, watch each step, yank the rucksack through the thorns. Does he know where to go? This is his mountain, but we are far off route. It's only our footprints in the moss. And on a mountain this high in the clouds of Uganda there are no helicopters to rescue explorers. Even rich white ones.

A gap in the trees ahead and I see it, dark grey. Rocks sharp, jumbled. For too many months, the rains haven't come like they used to, Solomon says. A trickle of water instead of a river. And now the smoke is on us. Run, stones slipping, my fingers reach to shake the rucksack off my shoulders. Solomon's fast but I'm keeping up. Don't turn back, it's raining ash and fear.

Then my mother. Christ, my mother! She's never with me, but suddenly she's here. Hands in the sink, staring out of the kitchen window. Red welts rising on her back.

Solomon is ankle-deep splashing, the water floods cold in my boots. We're sliding, falling, get up on the bank, it's easier. The breeze twists and it's on my face. It cools my cheeks, my forehead. It's no longer chasing fire down our backs. Our running slows and we stride strong and breathe deep. Keep it steady. We need to pace ourselves. It took three days to climb this high and now we have hours, maybe, to get out.

We can make the village before night, Solomon says, and I nod but we both know; we are at the mercy of the wind. One more twist and it will funnel the flames towards us faster than we can run. My body is not as strong as his; it reeks of office life and city gym rather than mountain trails, yet determination keeps me close, my footsteps matching his. I gasp the air clogged heavy with heat and dust. And a smell.

The smell of my parent's garden.

It's the summer of yellow grass and endless sun. I hide in the shade of my den, with paper thin strips of white bark in my hand. Each strip carefully peeled from my tree, exposing its trunk, shiny and soft, and red like blood.

The river turns steep into a valley and we descend without stopping to think where it leads. The smoke shadows the sun into too early dusk and I dread the dark, of looking up and seeing nothing but red heat glowing closer. I used to wonder if I would turn to God when I feared death. But the idea seems foolish now. If there is a God behind this destruction, it's a vengeful angry spirit. Not one that will respond to my belated cries for help.

Solomon waves me forward to a path cut through the undergrowth. A hunter's route that could lead us through the forest. Our steps become easier on solid trodden ground. But the memories scratch louder and louder in my head.

I'm in the garden: heat, no rain, and mother's there. She's in my den; I trust her. We sit either side of my tree, wrapped in its musky medicine scent. She tells me it's a Gum tree, a River Red Gum, and I hug it's peeling fragrant trunk. But then we're no longer there. We're in the kitchen, her hands in the sink, my fists pummel red into her back. The chainsaw whines and the River Red is falling. Finger thin leaves of green scatter. My den wrenched open, exposed. Betrayed.

Solomon waits ahead, he holds his water bottle out and I gulp it empty. Below, the river snakes towards villages barely visible on the horizon. Two days ago, we stood in lush meadows of vivid green and I itched to climb higher, to reach the forests where the chameleons live, to begin my research. Now we look out onto a patchwork of fields scorched charcoal black, shimmering with heat. And I can't escape the smell. The unmistakable scent.

The River Red Gum.

My den. My tree smashing into dirt.

In the kitchen my fists slam into my mother's back. My tree falls and she turns and grabs me tight. I should never have let her in. Gum trees love fire, she says, they are full of oil, ready to set alight, she tells me, but I won't listen. She is shouting, but my screams are louder. They burn everything nearby to make space for their seedlings, she says shaking me hard, but I won't stop. It's too dangerous to grow near our house. I have to do this, she says over and over, but I hear nothing except hatred boiling hot in my ears.

A gathering of River Red Gums. The villagers must grow them down in the valley. They are the perfect fast-growing firewood, but with no rain in this tropical heat they suddenly become an army born to burn. Each tree ready to sacrifice itself for its youngsters. Their parental devotion consumes hillsides of soft heathers, tiny chameleons and sunbirds. Life, soft and sheltered, unready to face such a foe.

By the river, I drop to my knees and plunge the water bottle deep. I watch the bubbles rise silvery smooth to the surface. Except for the rippling current, everything is quiet. No bird songs. No insects. Solomon crouches beside me and takes the overflowing bottle from my hand. I feel him lift me gently to my feet.

We must keep going, he says. My phone is in my bag, I say, and he shrugs; there is no reception until we reach the village. But my phone is in my bag, I repeat and I look back to where we came. Solomon's arm links through mine. I will find you a phone, it's not a problem in the village.

My legs stumble towards the charred valley, towards the drifting smoke. I have to believe we can make it. I try to imagine us already there, safe in the village. In my hands is the phone he will find for me.

I don't have her number, but it's deep in me somewhere.

My fingers will remember.

Mum, mum it's me.

Can you hear me?

I want to come home, mum. I want to come home.

*A single blow of a blacksmith is equal to
a hundred blows of a goldsmith.*

~ INDIAN PROVERB

Esau's Gift

By Chloe Headdon

The iron rod cooled rapidly, colour dulling from blazing white-yellow to orange, grey scales flaking from the glowing core with every strike. Esau itched to work faster – it would be sunrise soon – but he kept his hammer beating steadily, bringing the rod's point down to an even taper against the anvil. This piece had to be perfect. It would be one of the very last things he did for her.

At last the iron stopped singing to him, its sweet-sharp note fading from his mind. Unworkable. Turning, he called to the forge; a tendril of flame rose from its burning heart and twined through the air like a crimson snake, tail rooted in the coals, head coming to rest against the rod. Soon the metal glowed fiercely again.

Esau allowed himself a small smile. Thirty years as Master Smith and he still felt uncomfortable using his powers around others; each new apprentice always looked terrified to meet the Elken's only fire mage, let alone work for him. Right now, though, there was no one to watch as he finished the taper and coaxed the tip into a tight spiral, mirroring the bracelet's other end. His massive workshop was dark and cold save for the ruddy corner in which he laboured. Down both walls, twin lines of thirty forges gaped like black mouths. His hammer rang loud in the near silence, echoing from every hard surface as though a dozen more smiths worked, hidden, in the shadows.

So loud he nearly missed the stamping noise outside.

Esau whirled to face the doors. The tendril's end flew into his outstretched hand and thickened into a rope. Clenching his fist, he raised the arm high, like the wrath-guard he saw swordsmen practising in the citadel's training grounds day after day. The tail broke free of the forge and floated upwards to write a flaming *S* in the air.

A whip ready to lash down.

The march of boots grew louder, clearly recognisable now above the forge's low, hungry roar. Esau's dark skin began to prickle with sweat. A patrol shouldn't be passing by at this hour.

Had he failed her already?

A man's voice barked an indistinct command. The first armoured soldiers passed through the sliver of firelight shining out into the street. Flashes of steel. A parade of blue tunics. Esau squeezed the rope so hard that droplets of flame fell, sizzling, onto his bald scalp.

The last figures passed by without stopping. The unit *stamp-stamp-stamped* its way onwards, down the hill towards the civilian districts. He just prayed they weren't going to relieve the watch on the city gate.

Letting the tendril shrink to innocent proportions, Esau got back to work.

Pale light was filtering through the workshop's high windows when a firm rap shook the door. Esau rushed over, the finished bracelet heavy in his pocket, and paused with one hand on the latch to compose himself. Outside, his housekeeper Rosa stood tall and confident, a large wicker basket on her back.

"Breakfast, master," she said.

"Come in."

The moment the latch rattled shut, Rosa slumped to her knees with a groan and eased the basket to the floor. "Gods must have given me strength! It's been a long time since I carried her…"

"She's no baby." Esau leant down. "Did anyone stop you? Ask questions?"

Rosa shook her head, flipping back the basket's wooden lid and starting to dump food parcels on the filthy floor. "There are plenty of servants up and about at this hour — not every master's like you. The guards don't even look twice at us." Finishing, she took out a layer of sackcloth to reveal a second hinged lid, two-thirds of the way up the basket's interior. Beneath was a small head of curly black hair.

Esau worked his large, blackened hands beneath his daughter's armpits and eased her out. Hephitae sagged as he cradled her against his broad chest, one hand steadying her lolling head against his shoulder.

"How long since—?"

Rosa stood, kneading one hand into the small of her back. "Half an hour before we left. The healer was right – didn't take long, but I waited an extra five minutes just to be certain." She paused, then with a smile added, "She made a real fuss at being woken up so early. But then I told her we were coming to visit you, if she was good and drank up. She gulped it down so fast I feared she'd choke herself!"

Esau nodded, jaw clenched against a surge of guilt. He wished he could have been there to give Heph the sleeping draught himself, but the timing wouldn't have worked.

Or that's what he told himself. In his heart he'd been too afraid. Afraid of his courage failing. Afraid of confusion, fear, or – worse – betrayal, being the last thing he ever saw in his little girl's eyes. Better to put her to bed and brush a kiss against her forehead, then run off to the forge like the old coward he was.

"Thank you," he said.

Rosa nodded, but her eyes were tight and there was a quavering edge to her smile. Smoothing a dark lock off Heph's cheek, she whispered, "I can't bear to think of her all on her own…"

"I told you, she won't be alone. She'll be with folk who understand her."

"But they're not her *family*, Esau."

"Family isn't everything. Heph deserves better than me."

Rosa's hand fell still against Heph's hair. "You don't

mean that! You know you're not to blame."

"Aren't I?"

Even a week later, the memory burned him as fire never could. What madness had made him bring Heph to the forge? He'd had his reasons, of course: it was Rosa's day off, and he just needed to check the progress of Captain Goodwin's special commission. Perhaps sentiment played its part too: the distant memory of himself at an anvil, watching his Da put the final, precise twist in a pot hook, beautiful in its simplicity.

Esau had told his youngest apprentice, Fergal, to watch Heph while he inspected the piece: an elegant arming sword with the quillons shaped to resemble antlers. He left the two of them perched at a workbench in the corner, Heph laughing her bright, infectious laugh as Fergal demonstrated a metal spinning top he'd made, letting it dance across the pitted tabletop and off the edge, then stooping to catch it just before it hit the floor. The boy had clearly missed his calling as a jester.

But when Esau gave his approval and handed the sword back to its relieved maker, Fergal and Heph weren't there. A panicked moment spent scanning the chaotic room revealed Fergal tightening a clamp for a smith whose hands were full.

And Heph on tiptoe beside an unattended forge, straining forwards to reach the flames.

Esau's roar cut through the din like thunder. He charged

towards his daughter, shoving startled workers out of the way, and snatched Heph up just as her fingers brushed the fire. Her cry pierced the sudden hush that filled the workshop. She squirmed in his grip, fat tears leaking down her cheeks.

But when Esau grabbed her hand to check it, there were no marks. No blisters.

There was something else, deep inside his little girl's chest: an awakening, as though her heart had been a dark ember until that moment, and a sudden gust had brought it blazing back to life.

There was no time to marvel. To grieve. With everyone watching he hugged Heph close, using the movement to disguise the hard pinch he gave her thigh.

"Dadda! That hurts! That really hurts!"

"She's burned herself! I'm taking her to a healer! No," he snarled, when Fergal started forwards. Esau even allowed red sparks to crackle over the finger he pointed. "You're dismissed, boy. Go find yourself some other work, if anyone else is fool enough to take you." He stomped from the forge, Heph's cries tipping into incoherent wailing.

Five years old. His own magic had manifested when he was eight.

Did that mean she would be stronger than him?

"Esau, listen to me," Rosa said. "If you really believe Heph will be better off without you, say it now and I shan't speak another word. But don't turn a single mistake into one that will last a lifetime. I know I'm not Jen, Gods love and keep her, but we can still protect Heph together. You can teach her to hide her magic, and I'll—"

"No. Doesn't matter how well she learns to hide it. Nox's battle mages will sniff her out, just like they did me."

"And would that be so bad? If they found out, she'd come to work with you. Heph would *love* that. I didn't know whether to tell you this, but you should have heard the way she chattered on about the forge once she got over her upset." Esau tensed as though he'd been doused in a bucket of icy water. "Yes," Rosa pressed, "and think! Heph would have something few girls can dream of. A trade. A purpose. She'd share the same respect you've—"

"There's something you need to see." He met Rosa's wide blue eyes. "This way."

Holding Heph carefully, he trudged down the forge and through a set of doors into a huge, gloomy space. The warehouse had no windows, so Esau conjured a magelight with his free hand and cast the glowing white ball into the air, willing it to bob along next to his shoulder like a miniature moon. As he led Rosa through the cluttered space, the light passed over crate upon crate of armour swaddled in cloth wrappings and packed in straw, freestanding racks bristling with weapons, boxes teeming with arrows and crossbow quarrels, half-assembled trebuchets and ballistae, blank-eyed chamfrons for horses' heads, and finally, in the furthest, darkest corner, a line of four metal wheels taller than Esau himself. He stopped there and willed the magelight higher, letting the light reveal the rest of the machine.

Rosa's gasp was quickly stifled. When Esau gathered the courage to turn, his housekeeper's face was nearly as white as the linen turban covering her hair. He didn't flatter himself that it was a trick of the magelight.

"What—?" Her eyes roved over the machine, expression caught between awe and horror, and Esau could all too easily imagine what she saw. To Rosa, who was no engineer, this wasn't a remarkable feat of design. Instead the enormous furnace chambers and fuel tanks must look like armoured plates covering slabs of muscle, the intricate arrangement of pipes, valves and vents like a tangled network of veins twisting along the machine's sinuous body. Most chilling would be the muzzle at the far end, which even he had to admit resembled a dark, gaping maw, the two vents above like empty eye sockets.

In Rosa's eyes, the machine probably deserved the nickname Lord Equinox had given it: the Wyrm.

The Elken High Lord had never been a subtle man.

"Does it… it can't… *breathe fire?*"

"Among other things."

Rosa tentatively moved forwards, peering at the glyphs etched all over the Wyrm's body. "I know these… They're magic. Esau, tell me this wasn't your idea!" she cried, rounding on him.

"*No!* 'Course not. But you know Nox. He's always been ambitious to the bone, and now his imagination's finally caught up. Guess it was hard for him… first fire mage in his service. Took him a long while to figure out what I can do. And while I have people I care about," – he clutched Heph tighter – "how can I say no? You know how he works, Gods damn him."

"I do. I do. I'm sorry." She wiped a hand over her eyes, shaking her head. "But I still don't understand. What's it for? We're not at war with Saraxia. We've done nothing more than hold the pass for years. *Decades*."

"And meantime, the Emperor's taken more and more soldiers away from the border to fight his wars in the north. Nox's been waiting for a chance to prove the Elken name hasn't lost its greatness. This is it."

Rosa slowly stopped shaking her head. Taking a deep breath, she held out her arms. "Give her to me. Let me say my goodbyes."

When Rosa had gone, Esau placed Heph in the crate.

It stood among a dozen other boxes by the warehouse's outer doors, identical except for the small *X* carved on one side, so Tess would know which one to open when the time was right. Every fortnight the trader and her crew transported weapons and armour through the Forest to Kerdan's capital, Silníath, where there was high demand for Elken work. This was the most precious cargo Esau had ever sent.

Once Heph was arranged limply in her nest of blankets, he took the bracelet from his pocket and slipped it over her wrist, smiling as it fitted perfectly. He could have fashioned something prettier in bronze or silver, but iron was his element whether he liked it or not, and it would be the best thing for Heph to remember him by. When she was older, he hoped she would understand what it meant.

"I'm sorry I can't go with you, little one. I think they'd notice if there was a box big enough to fit me…" His voice cracked – why was he making jokes at a time like this? Stupid old fool. "Fire will always rule you," he tried again, laying a hand on Heph's hair. "But at least now you can choose how you use it. Choose something good. Something worthy of your heart. And, Gods be kind, maybe one day I'll make it to Carmallon myself. They say it's always summer there – their Elemental mages do some trick with the weather… We'd both like the warmth, wouldn't we?"

His throat closed up, sealed by a swell of fear. So much was beyond his control. Was Tess even telling the truth about knowing Carmallon's location? The magical community was supposedly deep in the Forest, hidden by magical wards. He wished Jen were here to ask… But that thought threatened to shatter his heart completely.

He fixed the lid on the crate.

It wasn't long until hoofbeats clattered in the street outside, accompanied by the low rumble of wheels. Esau heaved the doors open as eight wagons rolled to a halt, flanked by columns of guards on horseback.

Tess led the convoy on her bay stallion. The trader dismounted with an easy grace that made Esau feel even older and wearier than before, especially since she wore a heavy emerald brigandine, mail and leg armour, with a well-used sword and several knives strapped to her belt. The rest of her crew were also suitably armed for travelling through the Forest – though only he knew how deep they'd planned to go.

"Master Smith." Tess clasped his hand; her sharp grey eyes scanned over the boxes. "This the cargo?"

"Aye. You get it where it needs to go."

"Always do," grinned the trader. She swung towards her crew, most of whom were hunched inside their woollen cloaks, hoods up against the cold breeze rolling down off the mountains. "Load it up! And don't pull that face, Niko, or I'll ask the Master Mage here to drop a spark down your breeches… *Then* you'll move plenty fast."

Esau stood by as Tess's team moved in, hauling the crates into the wagons – not so much carts as strongboxes on wheels, with solid wooden walls and heavy rear doors secured with padlocks. Heph's crate went into the fifth, and he winced at how roughly they handled it. But it was better that way; Nox had eyes and ears everywhere.

Too soon Tess touched two fingers to her temple in a salute. "You have a pleasant day now."

Esau opened his mouth but she was already striding away, signalling briskly. The convoy clattered back into motion, echoing off the hulking storehouses lining the street. He stared after Heph's wagon as it rolled down the hill. The band around his chest squeezed like a vice. His eyes began to burn.

"Um… sir?"

Esau jumped. Fergal had appeared behind him, silent as a ghost. Of course, the boy knew this was when the shipment went out. He'd known to find Esau here, alone.

"Sir," Fergal said, drawing a shaky breath, "beggin' your pardon, but I've come to ask if I might have my position back. Work's hard to come by, and people have been talking, and—"

"You shouldn't be here."

Fergal flinched. "I don't mean any disrespect, sir. I just thought, if I came and spoke with you, you might—"

"Forgive you for breaking my trust?"

Fergal's eyes dropped, and Esau cursed himself for letting fear sharpen his tongue again. He could make amends. Take the boy back. But leniency could be treacherous in a place like this, where the smallest of actions were weighed and judged. What if Nox realised the truth: that Heph had never been in any danger at all?

"I'm sorry, Fergal, but I can't help you." The first wagon was already rounding the corner; he needed to get going. "You should head home. Go on, out," he ordered, when Fergal didn't budge. At last the boy slouched from the warehouse. Esau wasted no time seizing the doors and sliding them in again.

In the street, Fergal turned. "Sir—"

"*No.*"

"—why are you crying?"

The doors met with a heavy thump, plunging Esau back into gloom.

The gatehouse was enormous, a solid monument of stone set within the wall that swept around the bottom of the hill, towering above the jumbled rooftops of the lower city. As he hurried down the main street, packed with civilians and donkey carts going about their morning business,

Esau felt a surge of dread. Over a hundred archers stood between the crenellations, steel helms glinting in the rising sun. Many more soldiers would be packed within the gatehouse itself. At least he could dimly sense the braziers along the wall, all burning low; he wanted the men of the watch bored, cold and tired, dreaming of returning to their bunks.

As he reached the end of the street, the courtyard before the gatehouse came into view. Esau's stomach plummeted. The convoy was already there, lined up before the cold, deep shadow of the tunnel, the huge gates like an impenetrable wall at the far end. How had they beaten him here? Tess had had several more stops to make… The void in his gut yawned wider as soldiers in blue livery swarmed along the line, pairs of men hauling themselves into wagons while the drivers stood by with the keys. Loud scraping and thumping noises came from inside.

Tess had dismounted to speak with a small group of officers. Captain Goodwin's golden hair stood out among them. Esau forced himself to approach at a normal pace.

"… *one crate of bodkins, three of decent plate, five mail shirts of inferior craftsmanship…*" Goodwin muttered to himself as he scanned through the convoy's manifest.

"Really, Captain, I don't know what you expect to find in there," Tess drawled. "Saraxian spies? Nox's silky undergarments? Must be terribly disappointing for you, week after week. What say we skip the fuss?"

Goodwin turned a page. "This *fuss,* as you call it, madam, is protocol, and you'd do well to remember your place."

"Oh no doubt. Thing is, my place is out there," – Tess jerked a thumb at the gates – "where you boys don't seem inclined to go. Don't you get bored, watching those trees day in, day out? Or d'you think they're going to… *sneak up* on you?"

"Excuse me, Captain?" Esau interjected, before Tess could goad the man into arresting her. "I have your sword, sir."

Goodwin's pale blue eyes snapped up. Esau attempted a smile, but Goodwin's attention had already fixed on the sheathed weapon in his hand.

"Ah! I didn't know you delivered in person, Master Smith. Take over," Goodwin ordered one of his officers, thrusting across the papers. "And be quick."

Esau caught Tess's triumphant grin as he stepped away with Goodwin. Halfway down the line, Heph's wagon jolted on its axles as soldiers searched inside. He willed his hands not to shake as he handed over the weapon.

"Let's see what my gold has bought me…" Goodwin unsheathed the sword, a smile curving his lips. He held the blade at full reach, letting it tip and swing in his hand, checking the balance. "Outstanding. Truly outstanding. You've outdone yourself."

A horse whickered nervously. Esau strained to make out the soldiers' muffled voices. Was that a noise of alarm?

"Thank you, Captain, but the work belongs to one of my best smiths. Niall's his name, if you wish to offer your thanks in person."

Goodwin's smile faltered. "I thought I paid for you, mage. I paid for the best."

"I've been engaged with the High Lord's business. But Niall's very skilled. I'd trust no one else with work like this."

"Hmm." Goodwin returned to his examination, frowning.

Heavy, clattering thumps as soldiers jumped down from the wagons. Magic boiled in Esau's veins like hot pitch; he focused on his breathing, trying to keep it deep and even. A single spark might betray his unease. He was just scrabbling for some other remark when footsteps announced the officer's return.

"All accounted for, sir!"

"Then open the gates." Goodwin sighed and slid the sword back into the scabbard. "It *is* a fine piece. Though next time, you might send the man who made it. Excuse me."

Esau stayed in place as Goodwin strode away, hardly daring to believe his eyes. A dozen soldiers were converging on the gates, working together to lift the heavy oak beam and drag the huge, metal-banded doors open. The widening gap revealed an empty plain of bare, blackened earth stretching away, and several hundred yards distant, the Forest, a solid band of murky green that seemed to resist the early morning light. A gust of air blasted through, and it smelled different to the cloistered air of the city: fresher, sharper, as though it carried the breath of living green things.

Tess put on her helm and signalled. The convoy rumbled forwards. Hoofbeats echoed within the tunnel, then changed pitch as the first guards and wagon moved onto the wooden bridge spanning the ditch beyond.

But he couldn't stand and gawp; he'd already pushed his luck. Esau forced his feet to move.

A horn blast cut the air. Esau froze, eyes snapping in the direction of the sound – not from the gatehouse, but up the hill. There was some disturbance on the main street. Horsemen, forcing a path through the crowds at a gallop, civilians and carts scattering wildly before them.

Goodwin and his soldiers were staring too. Most of them. A few had swung towards the Forest, as though expecting to see enemies erupting from the trees' dark eaves.

The horn blared again. Esau's stomach swooped. Six riders, five in black.

Black, with blood red antlers on their chests.

"*Go!*" someone yelled.

Along the convoy, drivers cracked their whips and riders spurred their mounts. The men who'd opened the gates yelled and leapt back, flattening themselves against the tunnel walls as the procession became a frantic, charging rush. A second wagon sped through, then a third while some soldiers still scrabbled for hilts. Tess's crew already had weapons drawn.

"Stop them!" Goodwin roared, raising his own sword. "Stop them now!"

Esau started running. Heph's wagon rattled towards the tunnel, jolting dangerously over the flagstones. He had to get to her. Swords clashed and screams bounced off stone as Tess's crew cut down the men moving to block their way. Soldiers poured down the wall's steps and from the gatehouse's doors, like rising rivers of blue in their tunics.

Something whizzed through the air. A moment later red spurted from the neck of one of Tess's riders; the woman half-tipped from the saddle and hung there, feet trapped in the stirrups, as her horse veered. Esau swerved to avoid being trampled. More arrows and crossbow quarrels skittered off the flagstones around him and punched into the wagons' sides. Two carthorses collapsed, shrieking, within their tethers; the wagon they pulled hit their bodies and bounced, keeling over in a crash of splintering wood and metal. Ahead Heph's wagon started slowing, held up by the fighting around the gate.

Esau flung out his magical consciousness, spreading himself over the wall and through the gatehouse, finding every candle, every torch, every brazier. Each fire was a spot of red light in his mind's eye, a brilliant constellation peppering a cold, dark world.

The flames sang to him. He sang back, breathing them life.

Archers yelled as the dying braziers along the walkway roared into full flame, pillars of fire erupting ten feet high. The gatehouse's narrow windows blazed like red eyes. The volley of arrows ceased, and before it could start again Esau willed the braziers' flames to divide, to grow, to seek out his enemies.

A mass of writhing crimson tendrils shot towards the archers. Bowstrings ignited and snapped, sending arrows spinning against the pale sky. Metal triggers on crossbows heated to a red glow; men threw them aside or off the wall altogether.

"Traitor!"

Esau dragged his attention down. Goodwin's pale eyes had found him through the chaos.

"Kill him!" the Captain shouted, but Esau kept charging forwards, pounding after Heph's wagon. It was stuck inside the tunnel now, a black, stark shape against the bright vista beyond. All around, silhouetted figures hacked and writhed as Tess's guards tried to force a way out.

Flinging up both hands, Esau summoned fistfuls of tendrils to him, catching the fiery ropes as they shot down from the walkway. In his grip they coiled and darted like biting vipers, felling the soldiers racing towards him. When Goodwin himself charged, raising his shining new sword – the sword made in Esau's workshop, by a man he'd trained – Esau simply wrapped a tendril around it and plucked it from him, glowing white-hot, like a toy from a child.

Goodwin fell screaming and clutching his hand. The smell of cooked meat rose from his gauntlet.

Red lit the tunnel's shadowy interior. Flaming coals showered from the murder holes dotting the roof, cascading over Tess's crew and soldiers alike. People flailed like dancers compelled in a hellish jig. Smoke rose from the roof of Heph's wagon.

Esau bellowed. Fiery ropes lashed at the soldiers clogging the entrance, wrapping burning nooses around their necks and flinging them aside. Releasing his grip, he poured his consciousness into the tunnel, enveloping every speck of flame in his will.

One moment red coals burst against the people below

in explosions of sparks, searing flesh and hair and singeing clothes. The next, cold black lumps thudded off helms; the glowing embers covering the wagon winked out. Instead hundreds of tiny flames filled the tunnel's cavernous space, suspended mid-air like magelights.

Esau held them for a second. Then he let them fly.

The sea of blue ebbed as every Elken soldier dropped to their knees, clutching their faces. Esau tried to block out their cries, tried not to smell their sizzling flesh as he forced his legs to a flat-out sprint, covering the final distance to the wagon. It was rolling again, the terrified horses spotting a way out of the killing field. As the wagon picked up speed Esau leapt, somehow managed to hook his fingers through the door's padlocked latch, and with the strength of someone who'd given a lifetime to the forge, hauled himself up onto the narrow footstep beneath.

Sunlight washed over him as the wagon exploded out of the tunnel and across the bridge. Hitting the compacted dirt of the road beyond, it swerved violently, almost tipping up on two wheels; Esau frantically tightened his grip. A dark blur rushing by revealed why the driver had turned. Bodies littered the road, some in blue, some in green and brown. Riderless horses ran free across the plain or stood idly among the charred tree stumps.

A horn blared. Through the deafening churn of the wheels, it took him a moment to realise the sequence had changed. Then he sensed them.

Five presences on the edge of his mind.

An eerie ringing, not quite sound and not quite silence, like the reverberations that lingered in the air just after he'd struck an anvil.

The wagon rocked and bounced like a maddened creature trying to shake him loose, but Esau risked changing his grip to spin on his perch. A wave of sickness rippled through him. Soldiers poured from the tunnel's mouth, some racing, some limping or even crawling – not to pursue the escaping wagons, but to get out of the way. They'd heard the horns too.

The six horsemen seemed to block out the shrinking light of the courtyard as they charged under the gatehouse. Esau sucked in a deep breath and reached, straining, for the smouldering braziers along the wall, over a hundred yards away and receding with every moment. Sweat slicked his forehead despite the whipping wind. His heart hammered. Further and further he pushed, until a line of dim lights ignited in his mind's eye.

Burning the bridge would trap half of Tess's crew within the city. But they were as good as dead, and the other half would be too if the battle mages got within range.

Esau called.

A violent jolt ripped through his body as the wagon bucked. He tried to tighten his grip but he was already tipping forwards, the road rushing up to meet him. He barely got his arms up to protect his head before he hit, rolling over and over, every inch of his body pummelled as though with sacks full of rocks. The braziers vanished. His head filled with roaring black pain. His skin was on fire, everywhere, but that made no sense. Fire had never hurt him. Fire obeyed.

At long last the world stopped revolving. Esau lay

battered and breathless. The distant clamour of fighting drifted into his ringing ears, louder, softer. The ground trembled but he couldn't remember why that mattered.

Heph.

Where was she? Was she safe? Groaning, he heaved himself to his knees, blinking against the crackling darkness that clouded his vision.

He was halfway across the plain. Ahead, Heph's wagon lay on its side. The driver was struggling from the rear door in a crouch, dragging a small, limp figure. Another figure in green galloped back from the direction of the trees.

Esau staggered to his feet. He started limping towards the wagon – he *had* to reach her – when thundering hoofbeats approached behind. Swinging back, he flung out his consciousness, but there was no fire in this barren, lifeless place, barely enough latent heat in the air to create a spark.

The battle mage leading the group extended a hand gleaming with steely grey magic. Nothing visibly passed through the air between them, but Esau yelled as wrenching pain exploded inside his chest; it felt like someone was squeezing his heart, ready to rip it out. He dropped to all fours, fingers digging into the earth. There was heat below. The warmth of soil and living roots which the Elken's annual burning couldn't eradicate. Clenching his jaw, he tried summoning it to him.

Something invisible smashed into his shoulder, flipping him over onto his back. A heavy pressure crushed his chest, breaking his focus. Esau twisted his head around. Tess was galloping away again. A small head of curly black hair lolled in the crook of her arm.

"Get her!"

Three horses thundered past him. The driver, sprinting away on foot, stumbled and fell; he didn't rise again. Tess kept hurtling for the Forest, but it was still a hundred yards away and even then, the trees wouldn't offer safety.

"Master Smith. I'll confess, I had hoped not to find you here."

The battle mage who'd halted stared down at him, flanked by two other riders. Esau didn't know the man's name. They all looked the same, with their black-and-red tunics and hard eyes. But one of the men – the youngest – wasn't in uniform…

"You have the High Lord's deepest gratitude, boy. You'll be rewarded for this."

Fergal nodded and tried to smile at the praise, but tears glinted on his cheeks. Esau choked down a sob. He should have known. The Elken had no place for laughing jesters – only weapons.

"My orders do not permit me to kill you right now. You can thank your gifts for that. But understand, blacksmith, your life is forfeit. If you continue in this disobedience, we will take your daughter from you forever. If *she* proves to follow your treasonous path, we will take her from you forever. You will teach her all you know, until the day she surpasses you. Only then will you be given the mercy of death."

Esau gasped raggedly. Carmallon's endless summer was nothing but a dream.

"She will be the crown jewel in our arsenal!" the battle mage laughed, and his comrade laughed too.

Arsenal.

Esau's breath hitched. The warehouse…

Letting his eyes close, his body go slack, he pulled together the tattered shreds of his will until he was able to cast himself outwards. Heph called to him – a faint ember being carried further and further away. With a wrench he turned his attention towards the city, pushing hard.

"Too much for you, old man? Get him up."

Hands hauled Esau to his feet. He sagged like a corpse. Over the wall and the strain was already like being stretched on the rack; too far, too much, and his mind would snap. But he had to keep going. He passed over bread ovens and kilns, kitchen hearths and candles in the lower city. The boiling heat of the communal bathhouses. The enormous hearths of the citadel's mess halls. At last, just when pain threatened to tip him into a black abyss, he found them: twin lines of red lights that breathed and pulsed as apprentices worked the bellows. Nearby lurked a dark, mute void.

A hand slapped him around the face.

"Is he conscious?"

Esau gathered the glyphs one by one. The sequence wrote itself in his mind's eye like fiery script.

Then, moving his consciousness forwards to touch the void… he released it.

A distant explosion rocked the air with a concussive *boom*. The hands holding Esau loosened. He shoved his captors away as the blast morphed into a deafening roar, like a whole army screaming as one – a terrifying, wordless war cry. A shockwave sped through the air, throwing up dust from the ground and punching through Esau's body. Then came the heat, rolling forwards as though someone had opened the door of a colossal furnace. He gaped up at his creation.

A pillar of fire had erupted in the heart of the citadel, a thousand times larger than the ones he'd created from the braziers. Higher and higher it rose, soaring into the sky like a beacon lit by the Gods, fringed in a plume of dirty black smoke. The whole city was screaming.

"What have you done?" yelled one of the battle mages.

"What I was asked!" Esau roared back.

Nox trusted his mages as much as a rabid dog, so it hadn't been a surprise when the High Lord had demanded the Wyrm be operated by any of his captains – good, loyal men, uncorrupted by magic. Esau had obediently added the glyphs, which Nox's battle mages had checked. Was it his fault they didn't understand the intricacies of fire? How those glyphs, activated in a different order, could seal vents and redirect the flow of fuel, turning the machine's awful power in on itself? His forge was consumed. His workers, too. They hadn't deserved such a fate, but he was done trying to avoid bloodshed. This miserable city always demanded blood in the end.

He called.

The pillar of fire bent and arced over the city, a great river of flame swathed in rippling currents. Hands grabbed at him, crackling with power, but Esau drew heat around him like a cloak, a shield. Impenetrable. He revelled in the brilliance filling the sky like a song he'd been singing all his life, and only now discovered the final notes.

His soul was in that fire. It would be his last gift to her.

Light drenched the dead ground, turning the black earth almost white. All around the air rippled like a vast mirage. While the battle mages and Fergal cowered and shielded their eyes, Esau stared after Heph. She'd vanished into the Forest, but there were the three other mages, urging their horses on with vicious kicks, trying to outrace the fire above.

The flaming river halted its graceful arc right above the trees' edge and started spreading, as though it had met a vast invisible wall. Within moments it formed a mile-long band through the air. Esau allowed himself a heartbeat to marvel at its dreadful beauty before he called it down.

The Forest ignited with a roar, the front rank of trees instantly transformed into frail black skeletons within the descending sheet of flame. He felt the fire's hunger, its furious desire to race through the wood, but that wasn't his will. Heph's salvation lay within the Forest. Extending his arms, he pulled the flame towards him with all his might.

Fire rolled back across the plain like a wave. The fleeing battle mages flared and died like sparks within the incandescence. Esau closed his eyes as the light became blinding, gritted his teeth as the heat rose and rose, like nothing he'd ever felt before. It *hurt*.

He welcomed the fire with open arms.

On the Run

By Chrissey Harrison

Cold. Hungry. For days now.

A golden flicker through the trees. Someone's camp. But friendly? Or not? My choice – risk it or freeze.

The campfire burns unattended. Unclaimed.

I crouch, numb hands extended toward the blaze. One moment to warm up, to melt the tension from my shoulders. It's a mistake; now I've stopped, I don't know how I'll get moving again.

A heavy boot tread and a gun barrel at my neck.

I'm too exhausted to be scared. "Just one more minute." I gaze into the flames. One way or another, I've run as far as I can.

Up in Smoke

By Peter Sutton

A haze hung in the air, dry heat tickled the throat with the pungency of trees burning. Fire scorched the horizon. Above, night dark clouds obscured the sun. Fat flakes of gun grey ash flickered out of the sky and Martin flipped the windscreen wipers on. The car made a horrible wheezing, thumping sound. It just had to last long enough to let them escape the consuming flames marching across the county.

Martin glanced at Gloria: 9 months pregnant, knocking back water, wary eyes searching the road behind them. They'd not seen many vehicles since they'd escaped, a few screaming fire engines, an eye-in-the-sky helicopter but no families or other homesteaders. Not for a long time. Their car made a grunting sound and there was a sudden thwop, thwop, thwop and it slowed despite Martin pressing the accelerator down, down, down.

"Need to stop."

"We can't."

"No choice."

Silence since they'd fled the scene, spare words and emotions burnt away. Martin stole another glance at Gloria. She looked done in.

"There!"

Martin pointed. Along the road manicured hedges appeared. A house. The shrubs rippled in the wind generated by the fire. Martin didn't wait for a response from Gloria, manoeuvring the car towards the hedges and the gate that came into sight. Maybe just in time or maybe a fatal collapse, the car gave one final shudder and shat out a cloud of its own. The noxious black smoke adding to the smog.

"Let's hope they left some transport," Martin said. He let the car cruise to a stop and once it slanted into the roadside ditch he took a large handkerchief and wiped his face. Even this far from the fire the heat got you; the smoke was worse.

"Stay here," he said and waited for Gloria's nod before he wrenched open the door. He looked back once, noting with satisfaction that Gloria had locked the doors, the wing mirrors folding back. Gloria leant awkwardly across the car and opened the glove box. Martin shambled towards the house.

The double gates, twisted black iron, with an electronic opener, stood closed and, Martin checked with a push, locked. He spied an intercom, strode over to it and thumbed the button. All the while he tried to see if there were any people here, unlikely as that was, or a car. The garage to one side of the house, no – mansion, he noted, also closed and probably locked.

The intercom crackled, fell silent. No-one home. He could climb the gate, but Gloria? Feeling a little foolish he thumbed the intercom again.

'Smith' had arranged the family perfectly on the sofa. Mother, father, young Anna, Anna's little schnauzer. Picture perfect. 'Jones' however remained an untidy and unwanted addition at their feet. Always ready to spoil a job. 'Smith' prided himself in his work and made a mental note to work alone in future.

Now that the family were settled he could work in peace.

The intercom buzzed.

The gate opened with a creak but the intercom remained silent. Martin gestured to Gloria to stay where she was and stalked up the drive. At any moment the door would open and there'd be a friendly face. Except that didn't happen and he reached the front door with no welcome. It didn't yield to a push. He shuffled past the bushes lining the drive and peered in through a big bay window. A sitting room, he had to put both hands over his face to see inside, no movement, but he thought he could see people, facing away from the window, on a sofa. He knocked on the glass but there was no answer from within.

'Smith' grinned. He could have let the stranger drive on but he was both curious and had a need now that 'Jones' was lying down on the job. He snatched open the door in answer to the knock on the window.

Martin jumped as the door opened. "Hello?"

A stocky man, bull-necked and triangular like a body-builder stood in the drive and casually pointed a pistol at him. Martin shot a glance at his car. The man noted it. Thankfully Gloria had hidden herself. She was as safe as could be.

"Looking for someone?" the man growled.

Martin shook his head and stared at the gun.

The man nodded. "Running will get you plugged," he said, voice hoarse. "Why don't we head inside where it's less smoky?" He gestured with the gun for Martin to go first. As he passed within a few feet of the gunman he thought about grabbing for the weapon, but the guy was professional, more than an arm-length distance.

Inside, away from the all-pervading stench of smoke and in the cool shadows of the hallway Martin breathed a little easier. Then he noticed the coppery smell, and the lingering whiff of gunsmoke.

"Down there, first on the right," the man ordered.

Inside the room Martin spotted the family straight away and the body on the floor in front of them. "Old Jonesy there got excited. You're not going to get excited are you?" The man looked at the body. Martin cleared his throat, "No, Sir."

"I ain't no sir but you go ahead and call me boss." The man grinned. "You and me have a little work to do, afore the fire gets here." He nodded to the shovel in the corner of the room.

'Smith' couldn't believe his luck. A young, fit-looking man dropping in like pennies from heaven. Someone to take up the grunt work he'd planned for 'Jones.' And, unlike 'Jones,' someone he didn't plan on sharing with. 'Jones' had only gone and ruined things by mouthing off in front of the family, which meant 'Smith' had been forced to sort that problem out. Like he'd had to sort getting them out of stir, getting them civvy clothes and getting them here and having the plan for getting them away. He shook his head, 'Jones' going ape when 'Smith' had shot the dog made no sense. Fucking yappy little shit deserved it. Still Jonesy paid, wouldn't be mouthing off ever again. He moved his gaze from the corpse of his former partner and back to the stranger to catch him stealing glances out of the window.

Keeping the gun trained upon him 'Smith' moved to the window and glared outside. Nothing to see.

Martin grabbed the shovel and walked ahead of the gunman into the yard and across a lawn into a stand of trees. Between his shoulders itched all the way. The man kept up a monologue.

"You's better than Jonesy as you won't be answering back. You know how difficult it was to get here before the fire? That was some slick shit and all down to me, not Jonesy. Yeah he did his bit but wasn't quiet. Anyhow you can dig just as well as he could of."

"Why bury them? Why not just run?" Martin asked as the man paused to cough.

"You keen to be a gravedigger? Nah, this ain't no grave, man. This is paydirt you'll be digging. Stop there, kneel down I got me some pacing to do."

Martin did as he was asked and watched as the man ambled over to a large oak, turned his back to it then counted out so many paces forward, so many left and then some more forward. He kicked at the leaf mould and cleared a circle of dirt. "Dig here," he ordered and then backed off, gun always on Martin.

'Smith' watched the younger man dig and thought back to when he was king shit and owned this very house. It'd all be gone soon, the smoke thickened and the heat increased. He glanced towards the fire and thought he spotted some movement amongst the trees. He narrowed his eyes and was about to say something when there was a *chthunk*. "I got something," the stranger said. His attention snapped back to where it should have been, on the job.

The wildfire tore across the land like an invading army. Gloria had taken a while to get into position; she swallowed her fear and snuck closer. Martin stood hip deep in the earth, shovel in hand. The gunman gestured him out of the hole and told him to lift the box. Martin manhandled one of those military strongboxes, green, metal, about the size of a small suitcase, out of the hole. Martin spotted her but looked away quickly.

* * *

He'd done it. It'd been a manic couple of days getting here but he'd beaten the law, he'd beaten the fire and he'd got his treasure. He grinned and raised his gun. Three shots. Tight sequence. He dropped the gun. As he twirled and fell a young woman walked out of the treeline, smoking pistol in hand, trained on him still.

"What's that?" she asked, nodding to the strongbox.

"Looks like we won the lottery, baby," the guy answered with a grin.

'Smith' coughed liquidly.

"Let's grab their car and go, the law can't be far behind." She loomed above 'Smith,' studying his face.

"Sure thing. Let's not get this vehicle shot up too!" the guy answered.

She nodded and walked out of sight. 'Smith' tried to catch his breath but all he breathed was scorched air.

From the ground he watched the fire approach, sparks swirled in the trees as the smoke crept ever closer.

Since the house is on fire,

let us warm ourselves at the blaze.

~ ITALIAN PROVERB

Heated Words

By Ken Shinn

It had all started gently enough. He'd been endeavouring to enjoy an appallingly cooked breakfast when she'd brought him a cup of tea. As he lifted it and savoured the reassuring aroma of Ty-Phoo, as he took the first appreciative sip, she'd murmured something in loving, silky tones, and he'd smiled. Perhaps there was a chance for them after all.

The vile taste in his mouth had told him otherwise. He'd spluttered out the liquid and set the cup down. She'd had a momentary but definite smirk on her face, but his attention was caught by the drink. Its reassuring mahogany hue was now the uninviting grey-brown of muddy puddle, and that was covered with a thick, blobby layer of mouldy curds. He'd forced a smile.

"Darling, I think that the milk's gone off."

"Really?" Her voice had been soothing balm. "That's a pity, dear. Remind me to get some more later. Although

I'm surprised that you were stupid enough to try drinking it." The balm was laced with mocking vinegar.

He'd made himself a glass of lemon barley water and forgotten about it. Milk did go off, after all. It had been first thing in the morning. Not surprising that they'd both missed it. Dinner that evening had been fine, and they'd even had one of their increasingly infrequent and ever more cherished truces, leaning against each other on the sofa as the television pumped out relaxing platitudes. The evening had actually ended in sex which they'd both enjoyed, as far as he could tell, and breakfast the next day had passed without any culinary unpleasantness.

At the end of that week, she'd seen him off to work with a smile, and an indistinct comment ending with the words, "Break a leg, George." Which was nice. He'd been strolling to the bus stop with a slight spring in his step when he'd tripped over the un-noticed broken paving slab and ended up crouched and cursing in pain with what later proved to be a sprained ankle. On top of that, he'd missed his bus and ended up in the office a good hour later than he should.

His boss had taken him aside and given a brief, pointed lecture on how busy things were at the moment and how he needed to be punctual. Yes, she understood it was an accident, but the bottom line still mattered more. He'd made his way home, still in a good amount of pain only partly anaesthetized by the four pints he'd had en route, two more than he usually had on a Friday evening.

Accordingly, he arrived home hours later than usual, expecting a tirade, but instead his wife had tutted in brief sympathy, albeit contrasted by a satisfied grin. The grin hadn't bothered him, in fact he'd been pleased about it. Whatever their disagreements, she was still beautiful, and – like everyone – more so when she was happy. Everything was at least okay – he'd had a minor injury, awkward but nothing terrible. It'd be gone when the weekend was over, and for now he felt simple pleasure in the continued lull in hostilities. Maybe this marriage could be saved.

Monday morning dawned warm and sunny, but she'd stopped him as he was stepping through the front door and handed him his umbrella. He'd asked her why, and she'd replied, "Weather forecast says that there could be some rain later. Don't fret too much, mind, the weatherman said that it's expected to" – a brief pause – "be spotty, George." A quick peck on the cheek, and he was on his way to catch the bus to work.

He felt the first mild itching in his face as he took his window seat and opened his book. By the time he reached his destination, it had increased to the point where he was rubbing repeatedly at his face. It felt lumpier than usual, and some of the other passengers were watching him in a way that made him feel uncomfortable. Perhaps he was having some sort of allergic reaction. A bad pint, something he ate. Trying to forget about it, he got off the bus and strode into work, focusing on the day ahead as a way of distracting him from the increasing discomfort. He'd got himself his ritual mug of coffee and switched on his computer before he realised that his co-workers were regarding him – some with shock, some with what could only be revulsion.

Confused, he'd excused himself and headed for the toilets. Maybe cold water in the face would help. What he saw in the mirror made him gasp. His face resembled that of the fifteen-year-old he'd been, during his worst battles with acne, but grotesquely worse. His chin, cheeks and nose were covered with angry red blotches, many of them swollen, a good few already topped with sickly yellow-white peaks of barely contained pus.

When he'd taken several deep breaths and returned to his desk, the boss had come straight over and ushered him into the quiet room. She'd been sympathetic, but her conclusion had been blunt. Book a doctor's appointment and go home, we'll sort the sick leave. Could be an infection. Can't be too careful. It wouldn't be so bad if his sick leave balance wasn't already in the red – the stress of domestic life over the last year had caused absences which, bit by bit, added up. This was another blot on his record, and these things could reach the straw/camel's back stage with surprising ease. He'd caught the bus home, too caught up in his worries to even notice the stares of the passengers.

By the time he got off the bus, his face already felt a lot better. Raising a careful hand to his features, wary of bursting any particularly ripe pimples, he could feel that they were already a lot smoother, and a look in the bus's rear-view mirror on the way off confirmed his suspicions. His face was all but back to its usual self, only a handful of blemishes left which seemed to recede even as he watched. When he walked through his front door, only some fading reddish traces remained. His wife had greeted him with exaggerated surprise, nodded at his bewildered explanation, and then gone to make some tea.

As he sipped, he thought. He'd always had a fondness for the old saw that troubles always came in threes, but in his experience, they didn't tend to follow on each other's heels so fast, and they usually stayed at a constant level of severity. What had happened to him had gradually but definitely increased in the amount of trouble caused. By bedtime, his face was completely back to its usual self, but he stayed awake for hours longer, his wife having long since retired upstairs, and he pondered more. And then began to worry. His sudden transformation into a walking disaster area wasn't showing any signs of ending, and if there was any possibility of it worsening then he needed to be ready.

It was as he reached for his whisky tumbler that he saw the paperback book by the side of his armchair, left there in a way that could only be described as deliberately artless – she usually kept the house spotless, not a coaster out of place. He picked the book up and read the title on the lurid cover. *The Book of Spells, Hexes and Curses.* Flicking through the pages showed him all that he needed to know – it was a comprehensive discussion of the titular subjects, including some examples of them, as well as a handy general overview of witchcraft and its potential. He'd seen himself as a rational sort of person, but he couldn't escape the fact that the book had been left for him to see. A taunt, a challenge, or maybe a warning.

Whatever the case, it disquieted him enough that he decided to take a day's emergency leave. The office should

be okay with that, and he needed to know what was happening.

Decision made, he finished his drink, went upstairs,
brushed his teeth, and joined her in bed. He took pains
not to disturb her. In the past, when he'd done that, it had
been from consideration, even during the worst of their
arguments. Tonight, it was from fear.

He was awoken the next morning by the sounds of
cheery singing from downstairs. She'd always had a lovely
voice, lovely as the rest of her, and it had been too long
since he'd heard it sound so happy. Having made a quick
phone call to his boss to excuse himself for the day, he
quickly washed (the bathroom mirror confirming that his
face was completely back to its usual self), dressed, and
headed down to join her, cutting through the living-room
to retrieve the book. The morning was hot and sunny, and
she was dressed in shorts and a sleeveless T-shirt, her long
dark hair tied back as she prepared an enormous breakfast. The song was *I Feel Pretty*. Lapsing into humming,
she ladled sausages, eggs and mushrooms onto two plates
before turning to greet him.

Her feigned surprise at his arrival was mixed with what
looked like equally fake concern.

"Darling! I was just about to wake you up. Are you
feeling better this morning?"

"A lot, dear. I've called into work to take the day off,
just in case." She didn't seem surprised. He cleared his
throat. "Actually, there's something that we need to talk
about." He held up the book for her inspection.

She smiled as she saw it. "And why do you want to

talk about that? I mean, it's only a silly book, isn't it?" The smile deepened into a knowing grin.

"Well… maybe. But I was just wondering – you're right, it is a bit silly of me – because of what's happened to me over the past few days. It could just be a string of little accidents, but they're not going away, and they're getting worse. It feels less like blind chance, and more like…" He trailed off.

She finished for him. "More like someone's put a spell on you. George, I quite enjoy the odd little game, but frankly I can't be arsed this morning. You're absolutely correct. I put a spell on you." She sang again, in a decent imitation of Nina Simone. "Because you're mi-i-i-ine! And I intend to keep things that way. This marriage isn't working out, love. Something needs to change. And whatever happens from now on, I get to call the shots. Any fool knows that it's best to negotiate from a position of strength – and mine just happens to be supernatural. It's wonderful what you can teach yourself at home."

Her casual bluntness amazed him. "But, dear – why? It's not something to do lightly, the book says that! Look, I know that we've had our disagreements, but surely there's still something left between us – surely, we could come to some decent arrangement like civilised people…"

Contempt sharpened her voice. "Oh, grow a pair, George!" Again, that odd emphasis on her words.

Suddenly, his underpants tightened alarmingly. Pain shot through his groin. He collapsed to the lino, his screech of agony sounding surprisingly deeper than it should. She leered down at him.

"Well, what do you know? I've just made you twice the man that you were. Have fun with your double dose of blue balls…"

He'd staggered to the loo. Sure enough, he now had four testicles, and the two new ones were so tender that it hurt him even to walk with his pants and trousers on. The effects of any extra testosterone he may have gained were overcome by the chafing, but he wasn't about to wander around the house with his tackle swinging free – what if the neighbours saw? Plus, what if she decided that it made too tempting a target? Another thought struck him. If she could just magically remake him with no more than a few words, then why didn't she just do that? Make him her perfect man? Sitting down to think in more comfort, he came up with two possible answers. One was that, maybe, she couldn't do that in the long-term. After all, the effects of her other spells had worn off quickly. Maybe she hadn't learned enough – yet – to make them permanent, or else she'd deliberately arranged for them to only work in the short-term. He filed that away for further consideration.

The second answer was more concerning. Maybe she already could – but she just didn't want to. Maybe the plan was to make him suffer. It hit him how strange this all was – this was the rational world, magic was supposed to be confined to fairy tales and films – and then, how easy it was for him to accept it. Once the evidence had been clearly seen and felt, it became alarmingly easy to accept.

His next thought was a sobering one. If this was going

to continue, then he'd need to be prepared. And the only way that he could do that would be to fight fire with fire. He needed to study magic himself, and how to work with it.

His extra testicles having duly disappeared, the next few weeks provided him with opportunity. He was able to obtain some useful pointers from the friendly weirdo in the local pub, after that any times that he was late home were due to him hitting the libraries to follow up on those leads. His wife didn't seem particularly upset by his frequent late returns: in fact, she was positively cheery. Then again, when someone had you completely at their mercy with just the right words, and a head start in knowing how best to use those words, it'd be easy for them to be magnanimous, and the sobering thought that this was so ensured that he did his best to remain on her good side.

He'd worried at once that maybe he might not be much good at magic and made the decision to practise as much as he could in one area only, that of fire magic. It seemed to be his best option, a versatile element capable of being turned to defence or attack as required. His wife's ability with magic seemed startlingly wide-ranging, and he needed to be as adept as possible in one field quickly. He started with basic candle magic: concentrating on increasing or decreasing the strength of the flame by willpower.

It took him a fortnight before he noticed definite results, the flames rising or guttering as he thought, and during this time he also – to his slight embarrassment –

found himself chanting improvised rhyming spells under his breath to encourage results. The odd thing was, they did seem to affect the outcome, which led him to understand another fundamental rule of magic: that words have power. Sometimes only a few words, and they didn't need to rhyme, or be arcane and esoteric – in fact, a direct command often appeared to work best. In magic, as in many things, simplicity was the best option.

Having achieved some success, he moved on to the actual starting of fires. A further week later, as his wife snored upstairs, he held the safety match and focussed on its head.

"Burn, match," he whispered, and felt a thrill of triumph as it fizzed promptly into flame. So, he could ignite the readily-flammable. But a match was designed to burn, as were candles. He moved on to practising with items which could burn, but for which that wasn't a primary purpose. Days later, he set a newspaper to smouldering, which quickly grew to a small blaze that left nothing but ashes. His growing confidence made him complacent, and he decided to see if he could set a bath towel on fire with his growing powers. He should have remembered that the bathroom is the one room in any home which might be needed at any time of day or night.

He was watching with glee as the first small flames trembled up from the wool when her shadow fell over him. Suddenly a guilty schoolboy, he looked up in dismay into those glittering green eyes. She took in the scene in seconds and fury shone in those eyes – followed by a wry, mocking smile. Her gaze met his. "God, you're so wet,

George," she exhaled.

It was like he'd been chucked in a swimming pool. He was soaked instantly from head to toe, water washing stinging sweat into his eyes, dripping from his hair and eyelashes, drenching his clothes and hitting his body with unwelcome, shocking cold. It poured off him in runnels, splashing heavily onto the towel and dousing the tiny fires, which sizzled into extinction with a pathetic hiss.

"Getting the hang of it, are you?" She smirked. Her voice shifted into a creditable imitation of Bugs Bunny. "Of course, you realise this means war!" She'd pushed by him, got herself a glass of water, and headed back to bed, leaving that threat hanging like a small storm cloud over his already sodden head.

He'd towelled himself off, headed downstairs, and made himself as comfortable as he could on the sofa. As he edged into slumber, something struck him. She'd been wearing a man's T-shirt. One that was noticeably stretched around the chest, shoulders and arms. He didn't dare tiptoe back upstairs for a peek into the bedroom – their bedroom. He also woke the next morning to find his clothes now dry, and to the uncomfortable feeling that war had not only been declared but would soon be waged in earnest.

His worries were confirmed as he hastily prepared to leave for work. She positively danced down the stairs, favoured him with a big, pouting smile, and chirped, "Ride free with the wind, George!" – again with that slightly emphasised voice.

By the time that he reached the bus stop, he was erupting noisily and uncontrollably from both ends. The bus journey was humiliation enough, but he had to go into the office. He needed the job, and its routine, to provide some stability to his days. The ensuing eight hours were the most awkward that he could remember. He kept apologising, and all his colleagues had been sympathetic, but the boss had eventually banished him to an unused room at the edge of the building with a laptop and gained assurances that he wouldn't try to take any more phone calls. The privacy at least allowed him, once he'd opened the window, to carefully practice his fire magic some more.

He burnt sheets of A4, Post-Its, and the cellophane from his cigarette packet, before lighting a cigarette without lighter or matches, ensuring that the smoke also went out the open window to prevent any unwanted fire alarms. His control was definitely improving by leaps and bounds, but the worry nagged at him, what if it wasn't enough? Having finished his fag, he sat down and pondered what he already knew.

She seemed to be adept with all manner of hexes, down to control over his bodily functions. What if she decided to stop his heart? It wouldn't matter if it worked for five minutes or five centuries, he'd be just as dead at the finish. He cast his mind back over the spells that she'd used, trying to find any clues that might help him – and that was when the obvious occurred.

He'd been a fool to overlook it till now. Spells were words, and words were power. And the most powerful ones were names. Every one that she'd cast on him had ended with his own. A tentative smile creased his features.

Her name. That oddly old-fashioned name in which she took such a determined pride.

Inspiration had hit him at the same time – he now had a definite weapon of his own to wield. He just hoped, despite everything so far, that he wouldn't have to use it.

The barrage of flatulence had ceased as soon as he'd left the office and headed home. He couldn't say that his realisation had made him genuinely happy, but it did at least give him confidence, though not so much that he didn't find somewhere private on his way home to practice his skills some more. As a result, a pink-orange sunset filled the horizon and dusk was just beginning to fall when he strode up the garden path and opened the door with resolution.

The resolve died as he was greeted not by his wife, but by a towering, handsome youth with a lion's mane of white-blond hair, the torso and sleeves of his T-shirt stretched by powerful-looking muscles. And, he couldn't help but notice, the crotch of his tight jeans bulging to match. The Adonis looked at him with scorn, then addressed him in a deep voice full of fake courtesy.

"Ah, you must be George. I'm Travis, pleased to meet you. Do come inside." His handshake was painfully hard, deliberately so. George had followed him with mounting concern, adrenaline gripping him ready for fight or flight. At least he knew now who'd usurped his place in their bed – and, the horrible suspicion gripped him, she planned to replace him in the rest of her life. Travis had shown him into the living room, then strolled over to his armchair and settled himself in it with a smug smile.

She was reclining on the sofa like a diva, a large martini clasped in one hand, looking and dressed like a super-model. Elegant, beautiful, terrifying. Not so much a witch any more as an outright sorceress. Her scarlet lips drew back over a wicked, pearly grin, and the words that issued from them dripped like poisoned honey.

"Darling, how good to see you. I see that you've already met Travis. Quite the stud, isn't he? No, don't answer. I know that he is. I've confirmed it. Ecstatically. Repeatedly. Over quite a few days, now." She licked her lips, and an arrogant smirk filled Travis's face. "In fact, I'm quite tempted to allow him to demonstrate his credentials right now, in front of you. But frankly, you don't deserve the privilege." Travis swigged from his tin of Stella and laughed.

"Yeah, George. A wife as hot as yours deserves a real man to see to her needs properly, don't you agree? And let's face it, you just don't measure up."

His wife looked Travis in the eyes, widened her own in theatrical awe, and drew her hands slowly apart by about twelve inches. "Fuck me, you can say that again, lover!" Her chuckle was openly challenging as she kept her hands apart and turned to George, nodding mocking confirmation of her gesture. "Yes. In every single way you can think, Travis is more than enough man to meet my demanding requirements. Not just twice the man you are, infinite times the man you are. As I plan on affirming again very soon. But before that, there's one small point of business to attend to." She reached over the padded arm of the sofa and produced a medium-sized suitcase with a stage magician's aplomb. He looked at it with alarm.

"You see, Travis also has a huge… bank balance. Mine isn't so bad itself. We've got more than enough money to live together very happily. And I know that your account isn't too bad either – never been one for spontaneous spending, have you? So, there'll be plenty for you to go to the coach station, the railway station – hell, the airport, if you're feeling extravagant – and remove yourself from our lives. Permanently. Find yourself a new job. A new house. A new wife, if you can. But just get out."

"You – you'll need a divorce!"

"Will I? Who said that I planned to re-marry? And I don't need anything more than I already have. You know what I can do, sweetie. And I can do so much more. I suggest that you leave before I decide to show you – it could become… damaging." Her voice softened, just a fraction. "I may not have packed everything that you'd prefer. You've got one hour. After that, it's goodbye forever."

He was aware of the quaver in his voice. "But darling, it can't just end like this—"

Her voice was ice. "Oh, why don't you just lurch off, George!" At once, his body twisted painfully to one side, wrenching out an involuntary cry of agony, slumping him like Quasimodo. Travis, who'd been levering himself up from the armchair, stopped and watched in amazement. She'd made her point. Best to acquiesce in case she decided to make it something fatal. Probably neither she nor her new paramour would be too squeamish. Step by dragging step, he hauled himself across the carpet and meekly picked up the suitcase before heading upstairs. With shaking fingers, he opened the case, found the few personal items that he also wanted and packed them slowly. Then he closed it, sat down on their bed, and sobbed to himself.

Her shout from downstairs snapped him out of it sometime later. "George – your hour is up. Get out of the house. Now." Pulling himself to his feet, he wiped his eyes, blew his nose, and picked up his luggage before heading down to the hall. She was already waiting for him, Travis hovering with awkward menace in the living room doorway. Leaning forward, she placed a Judas kiss peck on his cheek. "Good luck, dear – and goodbye."

The door was shut behind him.

He made his way to the end of the road, turning back to look at the home that he'd lost, the life that he'd known. His gait was painful, but bearable if he held the case on the correct side. Doubtless the effects of her spell would pass, given some more time. Just like the lethal spells which she could still choose to deploy, and for all that he knew she may yet do. Those were the deciding factors. The fact that she had the power of life or death over him, and that nagging truth. A spell might be over quickly, but its effects would endure.

He waited and deliberated for long minutes, until the bedroom light was switched off. The only illumination in there now would be the romantic ambience of the setting sun, giving way to the sensual semi-darkness of a hot summer night.

He thought of her name. Of that silly, old-fashioned name that she wore with such defiance, the flaw that offset her beauty. The name that he'd not dared use for what seemed so long now, hoping in vain that endearments might ease the situation. There was no way back left. And, as he'd painfully learned, names had power.

He closed his eyes. Took the deep breaths of a diver, bracing himself. And whispered the two words.

"Flaming Nora."

As the erupting tongues of fire rose in the opened upstairs window, accompanied by screams of surprise and pain, he hefted his suitcase and hobbled off towards whatever life still held.

The Crucible

By Barry Hollow

I salivate, shorten breath,
eager and ready for the lure
of salacious language
you pour into me and solicit,
complicit in knowing your relationship
with the truth is not exclusive.

And I close lips, hold syllables in,
feel spice and excitement,
enticement of cinnamon,
nibbling nuanced expressions.
And they tingle.

As I push the nouns around,
taste buds primed
for a sultry tango of Argentine Malbec,
tantalising, tangled, greedy gauchos
gouge phrases into my throat;
knowing the plump, plum seduction
has fooled me with its glamour.

My tongue smacks, click-clacks,
after-tasting, acid snacks,
as your dancing deceit
dives into my fiery belly,
stoking the furnace,
fanning furious flames,
under this crucible.

This malicious meal of lies
now molten and simmering,
bubbling and building
to a steady timpani tempest,
releasing rage with explosive force!

Your hollow cremated carcass
now knows, this body rejects
the poisoned words you fed me.

My palate is cleansed.

*It is an ill procession where
the devil holds the candle.*

~ ENGLISH PROVERB

Sin Night

By M. E. Rodman

The bells tolled sunset.

Vis entered the sanctum. The windowless room blazed with light, row upon row of candles lacing the heavy air with the scent of beeswax. Around the curving walls and across the high, arched ceiling, perfectly polished mirrors reflected each flame. They flickered in narrow rows that criss-crossed the circular room, like a map of distant and dangerous stars.

Vis walked the maze barefoot. She wore the white of a Guardian, for that was her role tonight, skirts drifting out to pool about her ankles. Her arms, back and waist were bare and still she was soaked to the skin, her lips dry. She had paused at the basket by the door, for a quick count of its stock: wax and wick. Each candle in the room must be replaced as it burnt down, for fear that a speck of darkness would enter the room and corruption with it.

Vis wiped the sweat from her face. One wrong move, one misstep and the cloth of her skirts would catch, the flame would rise, devouring as all fire devoured, cleansing as all flame cleaned. Sin and corruption gone.

Vis had been dancing labyrinths since childhood. Taken in by the precept as a child, the sisters and brothers brought her up, gave her a place and a purpose. She loved them for that.

This year was the first she had been chosen to stand Guardian.

There, two candles to the left: melted wax and a flicker of flame. She leant over, heat searing along her arms, lit the new candle with the old, placing one in the melted runnel of the other. For a moment the flame flickered wildly, and Vis held her breath, not daring to move or speak or think. If it went out…

The candle steadied, flaring as if caught and held in some constant breeze and Vis let out a breath almost as hot as the air about her.

She followed the steps of the dance back to the door on the edge of the room and chose a fresh candle from the basket. The holiness of the sanctum rose up around her in heat and the light – fire and air as fierce as life.

Another dipping candle, on the far side of the room. Vis moved as quickly as she dared. Whirling through the labyrinth on speeding feet, fleeting tongues of heat on her ankles. She knew from painful experience that if she danced too close or paused too long, the heat would leave tiny, pink-white scars on her skin. The price of dancing the flames and a test. Failure to manage the swirling yards of skirt proved you were not skilled enough for the brethren's most sacred duty. Vis's hands were the same, a hundred tiny sparks of silver-pink, a hundred minute burns from taking too long to place a new candle. A legacy of the years of training that had brought her to this moment.

She made it across the room just in time. Ignoring the sliver of flame that shivered across her palm and the faint scent of seared skin, she lowered the candle into place. The dimness caused by even one extinguished flame was enough to open the way for the Everdark and its corruption. Keeping every candle lit – that was all that mattered.

A knock boomed from the heavy bronze door. Vis froze. Echoes reverberated through the searing air. Who would be knocking on this door, on this of all nights? Who would dare?

When the knock came a second time, Vis crossed the room, turned the latch and pushed the door open. A swirl of cool air fanned across her face as a flood of light and heat rushed to fill the room beyond.

It should have been empty, penitents spent Sin Night in Regent's Square, kneeling beneath the dark, moonless sky. Light from the Labyrinth illuminated two figures on the hard stone steps that led down into outer hall. A tall girl in the plain blue garb of a novice and, head bowed, a kneeling figure.

Vis stepped through the door, closing it carefully behind her to keep out draughts.

She frowned down at them. "What is this?"

The novice bobbed her head, not meeting Vis's gaze. "I beg your pardon, Sister."

"Do you?" Vis did not bother to keep the reproof from her tone and felt a surge of sinful satisfaction when the novice flushed.

"Sister Aven sent me," the novice continued. "This penitent is not permitted to join the devout in their supplications and yet is in great need of penance. Sister Aven asks that you allow them to remain here until sunrise."

Vis glared down at the novice. "Does the sister not understand the task I perform? Does she not value its purpose?"

The novice bowed her head in supplication. She was a plump little nothing, bound, no doubt, for nowhere more taxing than laundry or kitchen service. By rights she should not even be here but in the Regent's square with the rest of the brethren, only the Guardian remained in the precept tonight. Vis dismissed the girl with a wave of her hand, turning her scowl to the bowed and silent penitent.

They were clad in rough robes and knelt, their forehead pressed to the stone steps, hands uplifted in obeisance. The poor-quality robes and bone pale skin marked the penitent as one of the Profane, born with the sign of their sin upon them, shunned even by the most wretched. The wide sleeves of the robe had fallen back, revealing blue-veined forearms and a swirl of ancient script inked in lines from wrist to elbow. A sin eater.

Vis felt a lurch of distaste and wondered at Sister Aven's decision. What had the sin eater done to risk distracting the Guardian during Sin Night?

Vis nudged the bowed figure with a toe, watching as their head bent further toward the floor. The dull pewter braeva ring on the third finger of their left hand marked their chosen *forma* – they – as the novice had indicated. Many aspects of society might be barred to the Profane, but the right to choose their own *forma* remained. Vis's gaze slid away from the extra joint on each of those fingers.

"What did you do?"

"Sister?" The sin eater's expressionless voice was soft in the wide echoing space of the outer chamber.

Vis's nudge turned into a kick, but the sin eater did not flinch. They did not move at all.

Vis sneered. "You are here seeking forgiveness for your actions. Penitence begins with confession."

There was a moment of silence. The sin eater's uplifted arms began to shake.

"The head of my house died," they said at last. "I refused to sacrifice my hand to guide his soul through the Everdark."

"You refused your duty."

The sin eater met Vis's gaze with odd eyes, one brown, one green, in a thin, shadowed face. "I was born a sin eater, *that* is my duty. My house has no right to demand my body as well as my soul."

Vis frowned down into the defiant gaze. "You were born Profane, a blight upon your people." She snapped. "Your house has the right to demand anything it chooses."

The sin eater almost smiled. "Sister," they said. "I don't expect you to agree with me."

Outraged, Vis shoved the sin eater back to the floor. Flinching at the feel of sinful flesh against her skin. Why had Sister Aven distracted her from her sacred duty with such a pitiful example of unrepentance!

She left the sin eater crouching on the floor and returned to the inner sanctum. The sin eater's transgression was grave. Not simply a refusal to do their duty but a defiance of their fate. Vis shook herself. The sin eater was unimportant; they had been too much of a distraction already.

Tonight, of all nights, with darkness overhead, the Guardian's purpose was most sacred, most necessary. If one flame should falter, one light go out, the Everdark would find its way into the hearts of the penitent and destroy the world.

Vis stepped back into the heat of the sanctum, into the flood of light that blazed across the room, a thousand suns reflected in the glass above. There was the shimmer of flames, there the bundle of candles in their basket and there a candle, at the far side of the room, about to gutter out.

Vis grabbed a fresh candle and ran.

She raced through the labyrinth, skirts flying behind her, feet pounding on stone. The hot air in her chest heaved and her heart thudded each time her heels hit the floor. She trailed sparks, barely noticing them from the corners of her eyes. Her gaze fixed on that single flickering, fading flame.

She was still three steps away when the flame went out.

She was staring straight at it. The flame flickered like a snake's tongue, slipping sideways as if bent by a wind, though no breeze passed Vis's face. Then it spluttered, sparked and was gone.

For an instant everything went black. As if every light in that windowless room was doused.

Vis's stomach lurched, her breath rasping in her ears. She blinked in the darkness, once, twice.

And then she was crouched at the centre of the labyrinth, a lit candle in her hand, familiar flames flickering all around her. The wax of the guttered candle was still soft and without thinking Vis set her lighted taper in its place. Completing the pattern once more. Everything was fine. Every candle was lit. She must have imagined the darkness. Her skirts smoked gently, but the flames that had caught the cloth had gone out. Her feet and ankles smarted with new burns, flecks of pinkish shining skin like the kisses of salamanders.

Vis stumbled wearily to her feet, limping back towards the door and the slightly cooler air that seeped in beneath it. She kept turning, checking the candles as she went but all seemed in order.

Vis breathed a faltering sigh and rummaged in the candle bag for the soothing salve she kept there. She winced as she spread it across blistered skin.

She didn't know what made her look up. Every candle flickered like a miniature star making the room brilliant. The mirrors echoing back each flaring flame.

Only there, in mirror at the back of the room, lurked darkness. As thick and furred as a cat.

Vis froze, fingers coated in smears of thick, blue-flecked cream that smelt of honey and lavender.

The blackness moved, parting like cloud, and behind it rose a dark road. A figure walked along it out of the depths of the glass towards her.

Vis couldn't breathe. A pulse thudded in her ears and the room burned hot, so hot.

Through a wavering heat haze the tall, thin figure moved relentlessly on. Vis glimpsed golden skin and hair bone-white as the cherry blossom that floated through the air like snow.

Its eyes black holes in a smooth, empty face.

For a moment Vis wondered if she saw a face at all or some kind of funeral mask.

The figure lifted its arms and Vis found herself caught in the darkness of those bottomless eyes. She rose, her body jerking upright before she even thought to move.

The golden mask-face twisted; thin bitter lips lifted in a sharp, hungry smile. And every candle in the room blazed.

Bow to me. The voice echoed through Vis's head, hard and sharp, as the wind before a storm. And then, more violently still. **On your knees for me.**

Vis felt her legs begin to bend.

The door behind her slid open, cold air flooding the back of her neck and something whistled past her face.

It was a splinter of stone. It hit the mirror, shattering it with a crack of polished glass and firelight. Mirror shards rained down on the labyrinth. Vis bit back a startled scream, hands pressed to her mouth. The mirror and the figure were gone.

Moments later, she watched darkness form in the mirror that covered the arched ceiling. She caught the gleam of white hair, the twist of sharp, golden lips and felt a lurch deep in her stomach at the wrongness of it. It walked towards her out of the darkness.

Hands grabbed her arm, hard, and pulled her backwards, out of the sanctum, into the darkness. The door slammed firmly shut behind her.

In the outer chamber starlight turned shadows into phantoms and a faint gleam of gold shone under the hastily shuttered door.

Vis jerked her arm from the grip of hard fingers and glared.

"What did you do!" she snapped.

The sin eater met her gaze without hesitation. "We can't let it in."

"Let what in?"

The sin eater gestured towards the door. "The thing in the mirror, Sister. It doesn't belong here, can't you tell?"

The thing in the mirror. Vis suppressed a shudder. "There are other mirrors, ones you did not smash."

"I know."

"It's still coming." Vis's mouth was dry, and she couldn't quite believe she was talking like this to a sin eater. She had heard that some Profane were touched with unnatural powers, a lingering effect of their sin. Did this one have such skill? Did they know things they should not know, see things no one else could see?

The sin eater eyed her speculatively. Their odd gaze dulled to grey by starlight. "It needed you to pull it through. Couldn't you tell?"

Vis shook her head. Her head was buzzing with panic. "Why me?"

The sin eater frowned. "You don't know, Sister?"

Vis swallowed. "Is it because I let the candle go out." The words were barely more than a whisper in the vast hall.

The sin eater smiled faintly and pointed to the door of the inner sanctum. "It's because you believe in him."

The door, like the precept itself, was ancient. Built by the Golden Lady herself, according to the records of the Empire; painted in gilt and once vivid colours that had long faded. A detailed picture of the holy family. The Golden Lady and her sacred son. The Lady appeared short, and round hipped with wide, golden eyes. Her son tall, and slim, his eyes, once gilt like his mother's, had been worn by age to black pits in the blackened wood, his hair the white of cherry blossom.

Vis stumbled backwards; hands pressed to her mouth.

"No!" She turned on the sin eater in a whirl of skirts. "You're wrong. If he came back to us, if he returned at last, it would be a cause for celebration, it would be the mark of a golden age. If it was him." She straightened, head up and proud. "I'd walk in there and pull him out."

The sin eater stared at her from out of those mismatched eyes.

"It's him," they said, at last. "It's the Prince of the Flame, the Fire of Truth, the Dragon. And if you want to go back in there and draw him from the mirror, there is nothing I can do to stop you. Do you want to?"

Vis felt again the weight of that voice in her head. Felt

the tug on her limbs as her god dragged her up from the floor. She saw the cloud of shadows as it parted before his cruel, hungry smile. She'd not felt joy or peace when she looked into the face of her prince. She'd not felt the rapture that heralded a golden age. All she had known was fear and the terrible darkness that lurked in his hollow eyes.

"No," she said, and it came out in a whisper. "No, I don't."

If that was her god, then he had no place in the mortal world. That truth she felt deep inside, where horror thudded against her ribs like a heartbeat.

"He's still there." She fought to keep her voice even. "He's just beyond the mirror. What should we do?"

The sin eater shrugged. "You expect me to know?"

"You broke the mirror."

The sin eater looked away. "I felt him, his hunger and I realised I could not let him take a living soul – not even that of a priestess of the precept." The sin eater sounded as if the discovery had been a surprise.

But then the sin eater had no reason to help her. This was Vis's fault. She had let the candle go out. The one duty of a Guardian and she had failed. She hadn't known it would summon a god. Her god. Or that his summoning would be something terrible.

Vis had been brought up to believe the flames of the sanctum protected the world from the horrors of the Everdark. Had that been a lie? Did the Guardian's duty really protect the people from their own god? Vis felt a shiver of coldness deep inside her.

"Maybe when the sun rises…" Her duty ended then, when the long night was over, and light returned to the world.

The sin eater frowned. "I can feel him touching, testing, pushing. He's not strong enough yet… but…"

"But what?"

"It's Sin Night," the sin eater said simply. "It ends in a sacrifice, doesn't it?"

Vis felt a sudden creeping sense of dread along her spine. Right now, Sister Aven walked among the waiting penitents in Regent's Square witnessed by every brethren in the city. She watched and waited; a red-hilted knife bared in her right hand. How much of the night had passed? How long did they have before dawn? When the sun's gold lit the tall spire of the precept, Sister Aven would use her blade, the sacrifice's blood spilt to bless the morning and sanctify the world for another year.

"There are two things the Dragon craves," the sin eater said, "power and blood."

Vis swore. It was long and low and vicious. Sister Aven would have been deeply disappointed if she had heard it. She'd spent years working to banish the roughness of the streets from Vis's voice and the bite of the gutters from her actions.

Her life before the precept often seemed so distant, she almost forgot it. And then there were moments like these. When she remembered what it felt like to be desperate and alone. To have no choices.

She could not see the sky through windows set too high in the walls, but the starlight was still strong. Not dawn yet…

"He walks out through the mirrors. If we destroy them…"

"It might stop him?" The sin eater nodded thoughtfully. "But if that is his only way out then it won't be easy. He will fight us."

Vis stared solemnly back at the sin eater. "Us?"

They shrugged. "There are a lot of mirrors."

And nothing to break them with. The stone the sin eater had used to rescue Vis had been a chance chip from the wall, a lucky find. After searching the outer sanctum and finding nothing Vis began to fear the two of them would have to use their bare hands.

Then the sin eater gave a shout. They had found the little alcove where the lay folk kept the cleaning stock.

Vis grabbed a broom and the sin eater a metal bucket.

Armed, they went back to the door.

The flicker of light beneath it gleamed. Heat radiated from the door and Vis lifted the latch with a sleeve wrapped hand. She drew in a deep breath, the sin eater a solid presence behind her and flung back the door.

Heat rolled out, roiling through the air. Vis felt it blast across her skin.

The light hurt her eyes. Flames flaring to three times their usual height. Every candle in the room towered to twice its natural height, even the ones that should have burnt out long ago. They wavered across the lines of the labyrinth, blocking the route to the mirrors.

Behind her, Vis heard the sin eater gasp.

She reached down, pulling up her skirts and tying them

about her waist. "Move fast," she said. "The quicker you are, the less damage the fire will do."

"We're going to die," the sin eater groaned. But when Vis launched herself into the room, they were only a step behind.

The air seared Vis's eyes, sending tears rolling down her cheeks. Everywhere she turned fire blocked her path. The mirrors still stood, folding back and back along the walls of the room. Reflecting Vis, the sin eater and the conflagration.

The god peered down at Vis from the ceiling, where he crouched, face leering and eager – waiting.

As soon as she looked up, she saw his twisted smile. Firelight flickered off his golden face.

Look at me, reach for me. The words echoed through her head.

"Vis!" the sin eater shouted; voice taut with desperation. "You have to move."

She dragged her gaze away, leapt into the labyrinth and swung her broom.

Heat licked with dragon tongues at her already damaged feet, but she barely noticed. She swung her broom and glass shattered. One mirror, two, three. To her left the sin eater did the same with the bucket, swearing and sobbing as they went.

Fire guttered and wavered, flames running along her arms, reaching out to devour her hair until Vis had to beat out sparks at the end of her braids.

But the mirrors fell. Crashing down in an explosion of shattered shards. Until Vis and the sin eater stood together back to back, surrounded by molten wax and scattered glass.

Bare stone walls circled them. The glory of the labyrinth diminished to a small, round, hot room – like an over-sized chimney.

Vis drew in a breath of hot, smoke-ridden air and looked up.

He still waited. His cruel smile, sharp with anger now as well as hunger. His eyes seemed bottomless. Vis felt the tug of his will and a sudden rush of strength as his smile stretched into a golden grin.

"Sunrise," the sin eater said.

In the courtyard beyond, Sister Aven would be lifting the ritual blade to the bowed throat of the chosen one. She would be driving it deep into living flesh, a gush of blood and life to banish the darkness.

The moment had come, and the god exulted.

Now. He said. ***Come***.

The ceiling arched too high for the broom to reach, too far for Vis to jump. She had nothing to throw.

The god leant over her, his golden face huge, eyes black as tar.

She glanced across at the sin eater.

"Trust me," she said.

She turned, hurdling the candle flames, turning again, racing towards the sin eater who had dropped to their knees. She leapt as if in the midst of a dance. One foot pushed off the sin eater's shoulder, sending them staggering backwards. Vis soared, flying skyward, arms outstretched. The mirror arched perfectly above her.

The god caught her, just as she knew he would. She hung there in his arms, feeling the hunger of him, like fire that burns and burns and is never sated... But Vis had been trained in fire. She danced the labyrinth. She did not fear the flames. She never stopped long enough to be consumed. That was the trick of it.

Vis pulled one hand loose of the god's grip and, without pausing, as if completing the pattern of a dance, she slammed her fist as hard as she could against the mirror. She felt the skin of her hand split, felt bones crack in a jolt of sudden, ice cold pain.

For a moment there was nothing. Silence. Stillness. The god neither spoke nor moved. Vis hung there, blood dripping between broken fingers.

Then the glass shattered. It fell like silver rain on the candles, on the sin eater, on the stone floor below. Darkness fluttered, swelling like a cloud and the god recoiled.

He let Vis go.

She fell. It felt like forever. She fell through hot air still gilded with falling glass. She twisted, trying to cushion her body, arms over her head and landed with a force that drove the breath from her. There was glass on her face, in her hair. Blood on the floor beneath her.

The sin eater crouched at her side, their face streaked with blood where falling glass had caught it. They held Vis's hand though she couldn't feel it. Above her a gaping archway of stone showed, no longer covered by glittering glass. And perched crossways against the beams, a great black coffin, swaddled in cobwebs and the dust of centuries.

"Is he gone?" It hurt to talk. The words wheezed in her throat.

The sin eater squeezed her hand gently. "I think so."

The light in the room no longer blazed.

Vis lay still. Beneath chilling numbness, she tasted fear. What price would she pay for turning against her own god? What would the precept say when it heard what she had done? Would it listen to her explanation? Had it really been a lie or somewhere in the passage of eons had the truth simply been lost? Maybe the darkness of Sin Night and the Prince of the Flame had always been one and the same.

Cool, sweet air on her face. The sin eater's fingers gripped hard. Vis felt afraid but unrepentant.

Bells tolled.

Outside, the sun was rising.

Evenfall

By Kevlin Henney

The first sun set behind the mountains before she turned to look across the plain to the darker sky opposite. A shooting star had appeared on the horizon. Rising in fast counterpoint to the slower evening suns, it scored a white trail across the sky, dividing the world above. One new star became two, became three…

By second sundown the sky was combed with light, tidy parallels painted up from the edge of the plain, over and down to a ragged leading edge that chased the remaining sun into night.

By the curtain fall of third sundown they had caught up, completing their arc across the sky. The gone embers of suns were replaced by a blue–white glow. It was not the loss of sunlight that chilled her skin.

When had the ground started to hum? She felt it before she knew it. She felt the fear before she could think what to do.

The children? She could have gone back inside to wake them, to take them to the shelter, to tell them everything would be all right, to again wrap the truth in comfort and lies while holding them tight. The false promise that they could outrun everything that had happened to them. Outrun a marriage divided by war. Outrun a war dividing worlds, engulfing family after family, system after system.

The hum grew to rumbling harmonies, the horizon's glow burst into a false and unstoppable sunrise that reached up to swallow the painted streaks and shreds of sky, overflowing and melting the mountain tops as it poured.

The sanctuary of this outermost system had fallen. An end approached her faster than sound. There would be no more running.

She would not wake the children.

Yesterday is ashes; tomorrow wood.
Only today does the fire burn brightly.

~ INUIT PROVERB

The Sancti

By Dev Agarwal

And we're running. Heads down, legs pumping. I've never run this fast, never known that I could. I'm in the middle of the pack, with soldiers in tan swirls of camouflage on all sides. Harnesses and D rings clink on their broad backs. I'm sweating in my inmate fatigues, the pack tight on my back. But I keep running, pounding down the gleaming corridor with voices shouting "*Clear,*" in Russian or English at each junction. Their pace won't let me stop — that and the whizz burning through me — the army dosed us all with dextroamphetamine. Right now I can run *forever*.

We're in the sublevels of Baikonur's command and control building. This was built by us, but the Sancti took it and reshaped it. They made the corridors into a world of antiseptic surfaces, like they practice surgery off the white floor. The walls are trimmed with gold — as if modelled on their own skin.

The Group Alpha soldiers lead me straight through,

ignoring turnings to living quarters, maintenance, or the ground floor exit across to the launch site and the Sancti's base ship.

"Move your arse, Liz!" Jace barks at me.

This is more exercise than I'm used to. I'm not as fit as her soldiers. I'm not even as fit as the prisoners working in Baikonur – I'm a tech, press-ganged into Group Alpha.

But I run full tilt. I'm dizzy, burning up in my scratchy fatigues. The world is a square block of corridors, brightly lit and painted emulsion-white. Here and there slogans mark the walls: *The Sancti bring us peace* and *The Sancti are the poem for humanity.*

Vasily, running as point man, kicks open a heavy door onto a stairwell. Inside it a forest of iron staircases confronts us.

We climb, stomping up steel steps to Level One, when an explosion rips through the building. An avalanche of noise hammers my head. The building shudders sideways.

As the noise of the blast fades, klaxons blare and the lights flip to emergency red. In the confined stairwell, the alarm's wail crushes my head like a battering fist.

That was our explosion. Our attack on the Sancti.

The stairwell dips and rolls with the aftershock. It's a forest of steel, as red as an inferno. Crimson soldiers swing their arms up, pivoting, grasping bannisters for balance in a red ink world that bucks and lurches.

Right in front of me two Group Alpha soldiers die. The shockwave kicks them off the stairs to smash among the gantries below us. The Sancti have killed so many by now, why would two more people count? I think, wobbling with fear and adrenaline.

I fight not to scream. I'm deep in Baikanur. I've been forced to confront the Sancti. And the Sancti are unstoppable, as relentless as an avalanche. I feel them, hurtling towards me even as we charge at them.

Vasily kicks open another door out of the stairwell and leads us out. Jace, at the tail of the squad, slams the door shut. Its thick insulation turns the cycling siren to a murmur. Still buzzed from the amphetamines, I follow the squad. The soldiers slow, crouched behind their weapons, snubbed Russian AK12s and Heckler & Koch submachine guns. Vasily glances at Morwenna. She's wearing the same rough fatigues as me – but *she* really belongs here. Morwenna is base personnel, a Baikonur tech, and she's been here since the Sancti's arrival. I'm a newcomer, a spy sent ahead of the soldiers to prepare for this assault.

Morwenna points right, directing Vasily to the Fridge – mission control. Vasily creeps to a T-junction. This corridor is neither the antiseptic world of the Sancti nor the steel landscape of the stairwell. It's drab and dusty, reassuringly human, built by the Kazakh state for the Russian space programme. This is the original Baikonur cosmodrome.

Another detonation shakes the building. Chemex demolition charges. That's the gift of another warband. Group Alpha is made up of Russian and Western special forces, and is divided into three warbands. One band targeted the Sancti's alloy tower in the middle of Baikonur. It's over three hundred feet and loaded with arrays of sensors. The Sancti use it to transmit a suppressor field. No aircraft, ground vehicles or missiles can penetrate it. But Group Alpha didn't come by air, or road. They *walked*, hiking across the hard steppe of Kazakhstan.

Either our soldiers have hit that tower or the other target, the Sancti's base ship. That thing is four stories high and created what the military calls a displacement field as it travelled across the dimensions.

A month ago, the squad leader, Jace, said to me, "Both those missions are crucial, but they're nothing compared to us. To *you*." Right then, I knew I was going to Baikonur on this suicide mission.

The cosmodrome's internal levels have been restricted since the Sancti's takeover. When their base ship crossed dimensional space, travelling through what our science team called the *Leibnitz Bridge*, it arrived in Baikonur, displacing an acre of the steppe. But it carefully avoided damaging the cosmodrome itself.

The Sancti. They call themselves a poem for humanity. In reality, they are invaders, steadily destroying us.

The Sancti popped into our world through interstitial space. Their mastery of this dimension meant that they could cross the gap in reality that separates parallel Earths, with a Leibnitz Bridge.

On their arrival they executed a thousand people instantly. That cured us of our sense of wonder at meeting beings from outer space. And we hadn't. The Sancti crossed *interdimensional* space. They're not extra-terrestrials, but they are deeply *alien*, all the same.

Jace stops me with a hand on my shoulder. She tugs, fighting the dextroamphetamine driving me forward. Her other hand holds her Heckler MP7. She lets the team stream ahead into the Fridge. She's protecting me – and the laptop – holding me back as gunfire barks inside the control room and people start shouting.

Her left palm squeezes my shoulder, my boots squeak on the lino floor, when a voice calls down the corridor ahead: "What are you doing?"

Fabian. It can only be him. His voice is distinct, vaguely male, scrubbed clean like a BBC announcer's.

Fabian is a cyborg and the Sancti's mouthpiece. I've listened to his orders and inspirational poetry for the ten days that I've spent onsite. Like Morwenna, Fabian was part of the original base personnel, and he was here when the Sancti first arrived.

The Sancti don't speak to humans. That's Fabian's job.

"TELL ME ABOUT THE POEM," I shout at him.

But I realise that Fabian is not down the corridor. His artificial voice has no depth. I've not idea where he is.

Jace and I scramble into the Fridge. Two Baikonur techs lie dead, hit by Group Alpha's entry. A lake of blood spreads from them, glinting in an amphetamine-heightened shimmer. The surviving techs are herded out of the far exit as I enter. Mission control is a wide elliptical space, radiating out from the watch manager's desk. Plasma screens stretch out to the sweeping windows that overlook the launch aprons. Resting there, primed and fuelled, are two Proton rockets.

After their arrival, the Sancti touched nothing in mission control, they were in awe of our tech. Our advances in spaceflight outstripped the other animal races that the Sancti encountered in the mirror Earths. We even outstripped the Sancti themselves.

Vasily orders his team to tip over the ergonomic furniture, building barricades before the two sets of exits. Then they slap bricks of Chemex explosive onto the doorways.

My legs start crying from the run. I shake all over, a tremor of nerves and the drug come down. A migraine hums in my skull. I'm on this mission at twenty nine, almost the oldest and by far the least fit – even Morwenna, starved by the Sancti – is fitter.

"What is the poem, Liz?" Nestor asks me. He's Vasily's second in command. He speaks in Russian. I'm fluent in it – one of the reasons why I'm on the team.

"Ask Morwenna."

"The Sancti *are* the poem," Morwenna recites by rote. Her voice is rough. Her vocal chords were damaged by the Sancti. They are tough masters. "Humanity is just too animal to understand poetry. We see violence and invasion where the Sancti brought beauty and elegance."

Nestor stares at her. The Russian soldier is squat as a shot-putter and his nose has been broken and reset many times. I doubt he has much time for poetry. Then he shrugs and sets up a Tesla coil behind the main doorway. Nestor is strong enough to handle the mech weapon. The Tesla coil has been weaponised by the Sancti to excite high frequency electricity.

Morwenna helps me unload my backpack. Behind an ergonomic desk I set up the powerpack, Wi-Fi, and my de-encryption software. Inside the Fridge, we're close enough now to connect to mission control's operating system.

I fire up my laptop – a milspec Toughbook – beneath the wide plasma screens that dominate the walls. I see the surgically clean corridors of the cosmodrome's sublevels. On one screen, something ugly and stained disturbs the serene white and gold hallway. It's a servo-mechanism, a Sancti device. Once it had a sturdy carapace that resembled animated armour, all shiny alloys and graphene carbon. Now it's a burned-out shell, staining an airlock door as it smoulders. Another warband must have destroyed the mech.

Further away, workers in fatigues cluster at the end of the corridor. A red light flashes above the airlock door set in the wall. The workers are gathered round a taller figure.

"Where's that?" Nestor asks, watching the screen.

"A sublevel. Five floors below us," Morwenna says. Her eyes are hard, staring at the broad-shouldered man at the front of the group.

He's a Sancti.

The airlock's door is a slanted hatch, septagonal in outline. It's an escape route from the cosmodrome to ground level. And once there, we know where he'll run to. That's why I've been on site for ten days, in advance of Group Alpha's arrival, and blending in among the prisoners. I've gathered information on the Sancti's routines and, most importantly, their escape plans.

Around me Group Alpha comes to a halt, bewitched by the sight of this Sancti. Even on a plasma screen, he radiates power. The Sancti's eyes are mournful. It's hard not to be overwhelmed by the sight of a Sancti. Their golden flesh swirls, more perfectly formed than human skin. Humanoid, like us, only *better*. They beguiled us. Our whole planet trembled before them – mistaking them for angels in the brief instant before their war started.

This one wears a transparent bio-envelope, blocking off all possible contagion with this Earth and the animalistic humanity that they found here.

Inside the helmet, his golden face burns with judgement. Burnished and alluring, he's almost a creature of fire made solid.

"Our invincible enemy," Nestor says sarcastically.

"We can't stop them," Morwenna says, "they're impossible to resist. That asshole Fabian told us that." She sniffs. "But that one's running."

Each dead Sancti means a hundred thousand casualties in reprisal – at least.

Vasily would know. His brother was a Baikonur launch technician. He died three months ago as a punishment.

I turn away from the screen just as Jace says, "Heads up. Detonation." She consults her military Timex, "In ten seconds."

Outside the cosmodrome the other warbands are laying more Chemex explosives throughout Baikonur. If we can't keep it, then the Sancti won't have it either. A very Russian solution.

I feel the exploding Chemex more than hear it. A double drum beat that booms through the floor. The shockwave packs more punch. The walls shudder. Loose grit falls from the ceiling and telephones and papers judder off desks. An instant later a giant's rumbling voice groans through the Fridge. A keyboard shatters, scattering keys like Scrabble tiles.

From the wide windows, I see the dull burned dunes of the steppe fashioned from the winds that blow from four corners at once. Closer to us are the launch site's bays, and the two Proton space craft. They are pinnacles of engineering, primed, ready to hurl into the sky, the human dream of defying gravity. Ordinarily that would dominate my attention. But right now, the Sancti base ship dwarfs them. With its arabesques and angled towers, it's as ornate as a Hindu temple. The Sancti built it on their parallel Earth – and they hurled it at us. It spun through the gap in dimensions and stamped like an elephant's foot into Baikonur. Both their warship and home, it houses all the Sancti on our Earth.

Now it's on fire. Smoke rolls out of the four story block of the ship. Animalistic humanity has risen up. The base ship's windows, gaping like mouths, pour with smoke.

"We did that," Jace says, watching from her position. She's a hard-headed leader, but she sounds pleased.

Even Vasily smiles. He faces the main exit, handsome and lean behind his carbine. When he smiles, he looks a Russian Army recruitment poster.

The Sancti have waged a war against us, but for them, it was accidental. They aren't here to conquer, they came to help. They came to *clean* our planet. Humanity, the reflection of themselves, fills them with revulsion.

If we are lucky, we can aspire to live as their pets or their cyborged servants.

After this explosion the Sancti's enforcers arrive. I hear

the heavy tread of their mechs in the corridor.

"The Sancti are not your enemy," Fabian calls out and this time he is outside the Fridge, with his mechanical soldiers.

I blink and fight to concentrate as I work the laptop. I'm surrounded by distractions and noise. The Sancti's machines tap the walls of the Fridge. The mechs gather outside, each armed with a Tesla coil that will cook us where we stand.

Nestor and Vasily have set up the Tesla coil that they scavenged during the attack. Together they heft the weapon across a table top, facing the Fridge's doors.

Sound hums through the Fridge till the walls shiver. It's not an explosion, it's the two Protons: their engines rumble, rising in pitch.

"What are you doing? The Sancti love us," Fabian asks in his uninflected tone through the closed door. I imagine his face, as impassive as his voice, a collage of alloy and human flesh, one eye human, the other a glass lens. Morwenna told me that Fabian had been driving across Baikonur when the Sancti arrived through the Leibnitz Bridge. The shockwave of the Bridge threw him off the road. What was left of him was cut out of his Lada and packed into a mech chassis.

We've destroyed the suppressor field and the Sancti's base ship. The Sancti have run. They've left behind Fabian and their servo-mechs to do their fighting. But with the Sancti, it's not enough to chase them away.

Fabian says, "They will come back to punish us." His voice is devoid of emotion. The Sancti left that part out when they put him together.

"Yield now," he says, persisting without any nuance. "Lay your weapons down and come out."

Fabian is the Sancti's public face. He recites their poetry and their inspirational ideals. He has told us that the Sancti are a poem, a gateway through the boundaries of human experience. All we have to do is submit to understand that.

"Fuck off, Fabian," Jace shouts back.

"You cannot win—"

"Fuck you, robot," Vasily shouts in English, "We are Spetsnaz."

Half of Group Alpha are Spetsnaz, the Russian Special Forces, the rest of us are from a rainbow of European nations. Morwenna and I are the only civilians. I walked in here, crossing the steppe by night. The Sancti were not interested in stopping lone humans wandering through the suppressor field. They kept a pool of labourers alive to work in mission control or in servicing their equipment. I did that for ten days until Group Alpha arrived, bringing my Toughbook with them.

The rumble grows heavier now, baser, rolling through the whole building.

Underneath that noise, the tapping speeds up. The mechs prick and probe the wall. Light and attentive, as if a spider scrambles outside, wanting in.

"How many are there?" Jace calls. She crouches by an array of more of the plasma screens near the main entrance. They shine with the smooth blue of dead channels.

Morwenna scrambles to the main door and snatches a look through its window. "Two." She looks scared but her nerve holds up. "I can't see Fabian from here." She drops behind a table, holding an automatic pistol that will do nothing to the ballistic carapace of a mech. But she won't allow Fabian to take her alive if Group Alpha fails. Morwenna is tough, unbroken by her months enslaved here.

Everything is happening so fast. My fingers fly over the keyboard and sweat slides down my face. The tapping is now rhythmic on the walls.

"You asked about their poem," Fabian calls out from the corridor. He increases the volume on his artificial voice box over the heavy steps of the servo-mechs.

Jace motions at me, turning her wrist – *keep him talking*.

"That's right. What did you tell us when the Sancti crossed space?"

"Interstitial space." Fabian is pedantically precise. He's also well back behind the mechs. He knows that he's vulnerable.

"You don't understand the Sancti, do you, Liz?" Fabian says. "You cannot grasp their beauty. Or that beauty is sometimes uncaring."

Code streams across the laptop and a backdoor falls open. I'm in and I start earning. "Well you said that the Sancti were a poem from beyond the boundary of our experience. That's right, isn't it? And it's worth a little suffering, eh, Fabian?"

I work the code, still talking, but really concentrating. The code is all there is. I'm inserted into Baikonur's encryption protocols.

Fabian announces: "They cannot be stopped. There

is no negotiation with them. You've managed to kill a number of Sancti. For that thousands of humans will die. But the human race will still survive. Enslaved but marvelling over the miracle that is the Sancti. That is something, Liz." His BBC voice sounds closer.

Nestor leaves his position beside Vasily and checks the Fridge's main door. Blocks of Chemex stud it like boils now. Satisfied with their placement, Nestor retreats to another desk and picks up an egg-shaped detonator. He looks at Jace. The mechs have stopped their approach. Group Alpha are ambushers, they don't wait to be attacked.

Jace says, "Give 'em the good news."

"Surrender," Fabian says.

Nestor shouts at Fabian, "Robot, listen to this!" and he squeezes the detonator.

I lift into the air. It's like being pummelled in a car crash of colliding glass and steel. The Chemex explosion is so vast it slams the hearing from my head. The transparent desks, the steel doors and the office walls rip outwards.

Jace is smacked against a wall. She sits up and sneezes bright red blood over her camo blouse.

I lurch upright, sluggish and drunk. I wonder if I'm permanently deafened for a long second before I hear, distinctly, Jace shout through the doorway: "Still there, Fabian, mate?" The doors and part of the wall are gone, leaving behind a million splinters and a jagged-edge mouth in the wall. I smell burning. Two servo-mechs smoulder in the scorched corridor. One is torn in half, the other is knocked on its side.

Further down the corridor safely tucked away, Fabian

falls silent. I can almost hear his mind working, gears moving in his blue ceramic skull.

"Status?" Jace asks.

Vasily almost answers, then realises she's speaking to me. The mission is my gig now.

"Forty percent penetration," I tell Jace. We've hit their tower and the base ship with Chemex. Now the warbands will do the same to the cosmodrome. Their next attack may draw the mechs away from us. Carefully choreographed, I'm in a race with the other warbands. My code, inserted into mission control's AI must reach one hundred percent before the warbands destroy Baikonur or the mechs retake the Fridge. Now I'm here, caught up in the fight, the Spetsnaz plan feels as fragile as glass.

"Sixty seconds till the next detonation," Jace says, consulting her Timex.

Crouched over the laptop, I watch the virus spread within mission control's architecture.

We thought at first that Baikonur held no significance for them — it was just coincidentally their arrival point. But Baikonur was always what the Sancti wanted. They carefully left our satellites in orbit. The Sancti arrived here with no knowledge of orbital research. Possibly they are a hive mind, with a strict hierarchy. Once they committed to exploring dimensional space they never looked elsewhere, never looked *up* until Baikonur.

"It's happening," I say to Morwenna. She stares at me,

expectant and determined.

Beyond the windows, red flame flashes off the launch pad. One of the Protons shudders and launches. The sky brightens with its flare. The Fridge shakes with the shriek of its engine. The Proton's solid fuel turns Baikonur bright with light. This is the Sancti rushing to flee. The exhaust gasses light up the entire room, first a brilliant pink and then a fading crimson, dimming with distance. The second Proton spews exhaust gasses and then climbs off the apron, thundering out of Baikonur. Its tail lights up the desert. The edges of the steppe gleam blood red.

The Sancti have run. Driven out by the Chemex's fire in their base ship, and out of mission control by Jace's squad. They've fled on the Protons. Fled upwards for the first time ever.

"Take the control room," Fabian says. He's talking to his servo-mechs. Reinforcements must have arrived. There are always more of them. Probes tap the walls just once before a more aggressive touch rips the wall apart. Sheet-rock and plaster burst inwards. Silver rivets snap through the air. The wiring inside the wall spark into flame. The mechs shove through the wall and storm the gaping doorway simultaneously.

"*Down*," Jace shouts and I cover the laptop with my body. A servo-mech swings a Tesla coil into the Fridge. I stare at the huge mouth of the weapon, aiming right at me. It's not happening. If I tell myself that will it make it less real? Make it stop? I cannot let it happen, yet I cannot stop it. The mech stares at me without emotion. It is impossibly distant behind the Tesla coil, and just outside the Fridge at the same time. I see no reaction at all from the welded steel and enamel face. Its single central eye locks onto me, glowing green as it focuses.

I smell the ozone of raw electricity as the coil builds in power.

White light rips through the room and Morwenna shrieks. She's a crucifix in the air, diving backwards, throwing her body between me and the coil's voltage. Her corpse slams the carpet, bouncing once, then lying inert. Her eyes stare without seeing, right into mine.

Vasily comes to his feet, filling the room with the scream of his Tesla. Particles fly from its oblate mouth and it staggers the mech backwards, its carapace shorting and turning black. A second servo-mech is at the doorway, smashing its way inside. Nestor fires his AK12 at it. The bullets scatter over its armour, spanging and ricocheting as he raises his aim, reaching for its Cyclops eye.

Lightning bursts from the maw of this mech's Tesla and finds Nestor. His uniform shimmers with a halo of heat. His face, never handsome, stiffens with resolve. He fixes in place, continuing to fire his AK-12. His uniform swirls with eddying curls of smoke and then bursts into a cone of flame. He never screams as he burns to death.

Vasily shouts and swings his Tesla sideways to the mech. The white lightning of their coils cross paths, sliding through each other. The mech's carapace melts into liquid and runs down its body. Its Tesla coil jerks, angling upwards as it falls onto its own segmented knee joints. As it stutters and dies, Vasily's face burns away. His corpse somersaults backwards. I shrink back from the cooked meat smell of his death.

"On me. On me." Jace is there, somehow still alive. She falls back, bringing four remaining soldiers with her. "Round Liz," she says. "Protect the tech." Group Alpha closes in, crouched with me among the scattered desks and charred bodies of our comrades.

Morwenna is next to me, her arms are still spread, as if she is flying. Her body is bloated with the heat of her internal organs. I'm surprised I can still be nauseated but the stench of burnt pork makes me choke.

Jace taps my shoulder. I remember her hand on my shoulder as we ran into the Fridge. Reassuring and firm, guiding me. Now concussion makes her unsteady. One ear runs with blood and her skin is pasty.

"Did you do it?" she asks me.

I nod. Then, worried that she won't see that, I say, "Yes. It's done." The Toughbook glows a solid green. One hundred percent activation of the virus.

Even as the mechs blew the wall open and killed Group Alpha, we passed a deadline. They could not stop that. Fabian and the Sancti did not know what was happening.

Outside, the remaining warbands set the building alight. A soft, continuous sound like drums beats from deep within the structure. The cosmodrome is burning. Red light flickers along the bay windows. Smoke fills the Fridge, a greasy grey the shade of unrefined chocolate. It rolls through the corridor like a storm cloud. It brings with it a soft, roaring sound, as if the smoke is breathed out by a distant giant.

Heat thumps insistently up through the carpeted floor.

The smoke whirls over the wrecked mechs. One had its spraddled feet stretched out as if it sleeps in a cradle of its own shattered carapace.

Through the corridors, I smell burning. It helps to smother the barbecue odour of Morwenna's and Nestor's bodies.

"Hear that, Fabian?" Jace shouts into the corridor. She sounds satisfied.

It grows hotter inside the Fridge as if some giant furnace door is swinging wide.

I imagine the sublevels catching fire, the antiseptic white tiles curling and charring. In a short while the ground floors will submit to the fire, the building's iron rebars turning pink, the furnishings and plaster glinting with flames. Anyone down there, Sancti or human, will scream, their brains baked hard by the heat. Except of course that the Sancti have run. They are headed into orbit and beyond our reach.

"Look what you've done. You've won nothing except a slow death," Fabian says. "All you have succeeded in doing is killing us all. The Sancti have escaped. Did you see those rockets? Those were Proton launch vehicles. Why did the Sancti come to our Earth right here? Why did they cross the mirror worlds at this precise point?"

I realise that his even, indifferent voice has grown louder. It happened incrementally, like the rising heat from the fire below us. Fabian crept closer, under cover of the rolling smoke. He stands in the ruined doorway. The soldiers bristle, raising their carbines to meet him. All of us want to shoot the traitor.

"The Sancti are masters of interstitial space. This is the fourth time they have crossed it. We are the third sentient species that they have encountered on a mirror Earth."

"All of them just animals, right, Fabian?" I ask.

He tilts forward, his hips rolling with an odd gimballed grace. His cyborg limbs are slender as a spider's.

None of the soldiers fire yet. They are too disciplined to give in to their rage.

"They do call us animals, Liz," Fabian says in his scrubbed voice. It's impossible to tell if he takes offence – he is still one of those animals, after all. "But this is the first time they found animals that had mastered heavier than air flight. You've damaged their base ship. You've got far further than any uprising against them before. But the Sancti seized what we know of manned spaceflight when they came to Baikonur."

The room darkens into grey velvet. Everywhere I look fills with smoke. The glow of the laptop is a constant eerie green within it. The Sancti's space flight code was beyond me, built from algorithms that are too complex for a human mind. That was the Sancti's true poetry, perhaps. But when Group Alpha brought the laptop to me, they also brought an AI with it. It's why Morwenna and Vasily and the others had to die. They got us this far, bringing the AI virus into the Fridge – into the heart of mission control. Human built tech fought the Sancti. That was our answer to the question of what we made of their beauty.

"Their command is off Earth. I thought you might have guessed that," Fabian says.

The Protons are out of sight now. Above the smoking

ruin of their base ship, and high in the perfect blue sky, the Protons' contrails fade away.

Soon the Sancti will be in orbit.

Fabian says, "You've killed us all, either with these fires, or with the reprisals to come."

"What do you think?" Jace says to me. "An hour for a heavy G lift? Then synchronous orbit and docking in low Earth orbit? The Sancti are going somewhere, aren't they?" She looks at Fabian. "That is right? They're not just running away from us, they're going *to* something, right?"

A mech behind Fabian fills the corridor. Fabian is a slighter figure compared to the war machine's brute strength. Jace watches it crowd the doorway. Her soldiers tense behind their weapons, alert to this new risk.

He says, "The Sancti are rendezvousing in orbit. They not only stole our tech to build Protons, but they also stole ideas from us. They learned how to build their own satellite. A home far above us – the first time Sancti have been off Earth. They call it Mother. Matushka in Russian. You cannot touch them there. And if you don't touch them, how can you stop them attacking us again? Mother makes them invincible."

"Yes, you're right," I say and Jace smiles. "Mother *is* what makes them invincible."

Fabian steps into the Fridge.

"You've killed yourself and every worker in this place. Every worker on this continent probably when they finish bombing us from Mother."

He looks at me, sees me panting in the superheated air. His face is serene. A ceramic and steel face built by the

Sancti. "I worked with Morwenna for three years. She's dead because she sided with you." He looks Jace over and says to me, "These soldiers did you no favours."

"I guess not," Jace says. "But then I'm a Royal Marine. I'm not here to do people favours."

Keeping her Heckler aimed at Fabian, Jace says to me, "Tell him."

"You don't want to do it?" I laugh. "*You* tell him."

"Tell me what?" Fabian asks.

"Liz here is an engineer," Jace says. "A guidance control and navigation engineer. Specialising in AI for the space industry."

I say, "Those Protons? On their way to Mother? They aren't taking the Sancti safely away from us. They're accelerating. They won't dock. They'll never stop accelerating till they collide with Mother. We can't touch Mother. But the Protons can."

I tap the Toughbook. "We came here to retask their guidance controls. Each of them belongs to us now. And they're bringing the war to Mother. We're going to burn the Sancti from orbit."

"Really?" Fabian asks. Then to my surprise, he says, "Hah." He can't smile, he can't inject emotion into his voice, but he can still choose his own words. He gestures at the mech behind him. "*Away.*" Obediently the machine swings around and stamps down the corridor.

I realise Fabian has always wanted to fight back – he just never believed that the Sancti could lose. He was resigned to his servitude. He glances at me. The blue and silver segments of his skull gleam in the smoke. "A poem,"

He says without inflection. But I think I hear something new there – his sarcasm.

"That's what they promised," I say.

Jace tips her Heckler back against her shoulder. Fabian is no threat. "Liz here just rewrote that poem's ending."

Together, we look up. The Sancti are still making their escape. Perhaps they're already planning their revenge. But soon they'll be fighting, trying to retask the very Protons that they're on. And when they can't, they'll watch Mother race towards them, ever faster and ever larger, until they slam together in the silence of the void. Mother will break orbit and spin about the Earth before it falls back to us, a flaming sword in our atmosphere. That promises to be the last marks of the Sancti upon the world, no matter how perfect and beautiful they are.

"Creatures of fire," Jace says.

"And they met animals that play with fire," I say.

Chocolate smoke swirls around all of us. Thicker, more velvety than before.

Fabian says, "Follow me out of here before all of us needlessly die."

I realise I hadn't thought about this moment. My mind had closed off any possibility of living past my one task. What happens after that was beyond my imagining.

"We carry our dead," Jace says. The surviving men of Group Alpha shoulder our dead comrades.

I straggle out after them, following Fabian. What is left of life waits beyond the steady churn of smoke. A world without the Sancti beckons. But I wonder if there is enough of me left to resume living in that world. I march forward, fighting my exhaustion and the come-down from the amphetamines, the fight, and the victory. The world will be filled with ghosts and loneliness, with warmth and light and, I realise, poetry once more, now that we have banished the Sancti.

With that thought, I walk out of Baikonur and its fires. I am at last ready to imagine the future again.

Life, like a fire, begins in smoke
and ends in ashes.

~ Arabian Proverb

The Heat of the Forge

By Scott Lewis

The drop of sweat took several minutes to form, before rolling down the blacksmith's wrinkled brow and dropping off the end of his hooked nose. He paid it no heed, concentrating on the glowing metal bar he held in his long-handled tongs. Unblinking, he waited for the right moment to bring his hammer down, each stroke beating the metal into shape. With every beat he exhaled, rheumy eyes reflecting the glow of the forge and exploding with mirrored sparks every time the hammer descended.

Too many years he had stood before this forge. As his father's apprentice, he fetched pig-iron and coke and worked the bellows as his father wrought tools, shoed horses, and tended the constantly-burning coals. It had been a hard childhood, and it made him hard in turn. By his eighteenth birthday he was the strongest of the village lads. His father would soon send him to the City to complete his training and become a guild blacksmith. He took a wife; nine months later she would give him two fine sons.

Inch by inch, section by section, the blade began to take shape. Each fall of the hammer brought it closer to completion. The blacksmith had lost count of the number of strokes. Arthritic fingers had locked in place around the handles of the tongs, but he felt no discomfort. Any pain he may have suffered when it first set in was long gone, replaced by the numbness of joints resigned to their fate.

The Enemy rose in the West six weeks after his birthday, sweeping down out of the mountains and overwhelming the border forts in a single night of epic violence. Only the valiant resistance of the Border Lords and Ladies prevented the Enemy from surging deep into the heart of the Kingdom. He would never forget the day the King's riders arrived in the village, demanding the service of all men and women who could wield a sword or carry a pike.

Using a long, blunt awl, he scored a fuller into each section of the blade. The long, shallow channel would add strength to the weapon, lighten the weight, and provide a channel for the blood of the enemy to run down almost as an afterthought. A gobbet of molten metal spat from the furnace, landing on his apron and his bare forearm. It scorched the leather black; on his skin it left an angry, red burn. His eyes never left the blade he was working on, the smell of burning flesh mixing with the smoke from the blazing coke, the stinging tang of molten metal, and the reek of the sweat from his own unwashed body.

Like his father, he had become a line-breaker; armed with a huge two-handed greatsword, he hurled himself at the Enemy's massed ranks, cutting through blocks of infantry or blunting the charge of heavy cavalry. His father fell to a lance somewhere in the Borderlands – he couldn't remember where. Battle ran in to battle, until that day before the gates of one of the great cities. The day where the tide had begun to turn.

The forging of the sections took his utmost concentration. Any misalignment would result in the blade being imperfect, weak; he couldn't stand the thought of his work being anything less than immaculate. Ignoring the heat from the flames he swapped the sections between anvil and furnace, the thick leather gloves protecting him as he thrust the iron repeatedly into the flames, softening the sections and hammering them into shape.

They had won a crushing victory over the Enemy that day, had halted their advance on the Capital. It had come at a price, however, and he was part of the butcher's bill. A blow from a warhammer smashed his leg, leaving him lame. The King had fallen as well; his daughter taking his place at the head of the army. They marched the next day without him. Once his leg had regained enough strength, he had made his way back to the village, relying on the kindness of strangers to aid yet another cripple left behind in the wake of the war.

His leg twinged in protest at the heat and the time he had spent standing. He ignored it as he ignored all of his body's other protestations. The blade before him was finally taking shape; under the brutal caress of his hammer and the crushing embrace of his tongs the weapon became recognisable, and eventually he was satisfied that the first part of the process was complete. With a grunt of exertion, he thrust the nascent sword deep into the hottest part of the coals.

The forge had fallen silent and cool with the absence of master and apprentice to tend it. As he recovered from his wound, nursed to health by his wife and entertained by his infant sons, he regained his strength. The Enemy was still strong, and the armies of the Kingdom faced a daunting task pushing them back across the country. When further demands for aid came from the Queen's riders, he rose from his sickbed and fired up the forge. Once the coals were hot enough to soften the steel, he made his first sword.

The blade spent a day wrapped in insulating material to cool. The following morning, old bones creaking with rheumatic stiffness and plagued by a hundred niggling aches, the blacksmith bent over his grindstone, spinning the crank with one hand as he drew the soft metal over the rough sandstone, bringing it to a perfect edge and a vicious, killing point.

Making weapons for the Queen's army became his whole life. He owed it to his father, to those who had fallen with him, and to those who could no longer fight. Stubborn pride drove him back to the forge, day after day. He stopped paying attention to the tack, horseshoes and other needs of his neigh-

bours; like many forges across the Kingdom his every waking hour was spent making weapons of war.

With a sickening crack, he stood upright. Placing his hands in the small of his back, the blacksmith arched backwards to relieve the sudden sharp pain in his spine. Mobility restored, he fired up the forge again. As he watched the newly-born flames leap to life, he worked the same bellows he had worked as a child, and then again as a man. With each compression of the rawhide, he grunted with exertion. He had no apprentice to work the bellows as he had for his father; all the young people in the village had gone off to fight.

His twin sons were taken to serve the King as soon as they could shoulder a spear. The war had been going on for fifteen years, and the battle lines hadn't moved for five. The Queen had died, sword in hand, fighting the Enemy's elite troops. One of his boys fell beneath the arrows of the Enemy's archers during a minor skirmish in the Borderlands. Maddened with grief, the other threw himself alone into an infantry formation. There was barely enough left of his body for the notifying officer to identify.

After several hours, he was satisfied with the temperature. The heat pouring from the forge was unbearable, inhospitable; his wife had always said she could never understand how he stood it. The heat was as much a part of him as he was of it, each scald and burn repaid with a mighty hammer blow or gust from the bellows. Thick, corded muscle glistened with sweat and reflected the light of the furnace, giving off an impression of youth and vitality and disguising the wrinkled, liver-spotted skin and the hunched, stooped figure.

A bloody flux took his wife quickly. She had never recovered from the death of their sons, and whilst he withdrew to the forge he ignored the fact that they had withdrawn from each other. He had held her hand as she breathed her last, but the woman on the bed before him was not someone he knew any more. He knew he loved her, but he had no real idea of the woman his wife had been.

Gripping the white-hot blade in the tongs, he removed it from the forge and drove it deep into a barrel of oil. The oil hissed and bubbled for a moment, spitting into his face and over his torso as it engulfed the fruits of his labour. In the barrel the blade would be undergoing a change; tempering and hardening and becoming an instrument of war.

He couldn't put a number to the days he had spent toiling at his forge, the number of weapons he had sent to the new King's soldiers, or the price he had paid to support the war against the Enemy. Faces from his past came to him occasionally when he slept, but he couldn't remember their names. His body went from tall, muscular and imposing to bent, shrivelled and broken. Each night his back ached, his hand took hours to unclench, and his skin was raw where it had not had time to heal. He had few neighbours now, and most of the village houses stood, abandoned and empty.

Once the quenching and hardening was complete, the last act in the creation of the sword was to apply the handle. He took two pieces of oak, painstakingly sanding each to a perfect fit. He affixed them to the tang with three metal dowels, then wrapped the hilt in the finest leather he had. Looking at the finished weapon, he allowed himself a crooked-toothed smile. It was a good piece. It would serve the King well, like his father had, like his sons had, and like he had. Now he could rest. He was tired. So very, very tired.

The young soldier found him when she came with the cart to collect his latest load of weapons two days later. He was sat in a rickety chair, a smile on his face and a newly-forged sword in his lap. As the soldier picked up the sword, a single ember from the forge reflected in the blade. As she watched, the ember cooled and winked out of existence.

Last Game

By Clare Dornan

Grandad's at the front in a wooden box, glossy and black like the domino set he kept on his mantelpiece.

We used to play on Sunday after the plates were cleared and the kitchen tidy. His curly white eyebrows twitching while he thought. Each piece given a luck spin before he laid it carefully in place. He was so damn pleased with himself when he beat me, it was almost worth letting him win.

Now the black box slides towards the curtains. The flames behind, ready and waiting.

"You off then?" I whisper.

That's what he'd say when I hugged his bony shoulders and felt his wheezing ribs beneath his thin cotton shirt.

I'll beat you next time, I'd say. Next time.

Long Hot Summer

By Nick Walters

It was the last one in the box. I teased it out and held it reverently between thumb and forefinger. So small, just a splinter. But so much potential. I threw the now-empty box onto the pyre. More fuel, not much, but it all helped. I glanced from the match to Andy. His blue eyes blinked, shaded by a fringe of brown hair.

"Go on then," he said, gesturing towards the pile. "Someone might come."

I scanned the lane to check, a watery feeling lurching in my innards. Beyond Andy, the lane ascended in a narrow strip of tarmac back towards the main road. No traffic could be heard. All was silent except for the hum of the sewage works. We stood on the square concrete apron that bordered the gates of the works, our bikes leant against the chainlink fence.

We were forbidden by our parents to go anywhere near the sewage works – they feared we would catch something – but the place fascinated us. It was like a strange, alien base in the middle of the countryside, with its windowless blocky buildings and circular aeration tanks with their eerily rotating scraper arms.

In the middle of the concrete apron stood the pyre. It was mostly twigs, dry grass and old newspapers, anything we could find we thought would go up. It was a hot day in late June, the sky above us cloudless, the heat beating down on the backs of our necks and bare arms.

And we were about to add to that heat.

The pyre was not large, about the size of a spacehopper. It was dry as a bone and we knew it would go up a treat.

I nodded at Andy and knelt before the pyre. Andy stood, arms folded, some distance back, and not for the first time I doubted his commitment to the enterprise. I narrowed my eyes at the match: it was a good one, stout, white with a bulbous red head. No doubt it would strike first time, but there was always that worry it would sputter out before it reached the pyre. And as this was the last one, this worry gripped my guts in a giant fist.

Taking a deep breath, I struck it in a swift movement on the gritty concrete, and with a crackling flutter, its head burst to flame. I watched it for a moment, marvelling at the beautiful bloom which was about to flower from this tiny bud. Then, still kneeling, I reached forward and introduced the flame to a clump of dry grass at the base of the pyre, bleached almost white by the merciless summer sun. It caught immediately, pale orange flame dancing and spreading. The intoxicating smell of burning reached me. I dropped the match and stood, backing off until I was next to Andy.

The distant grumble of a lorry or bus on the main road startled us, but it was quickly gone and our attention returned to the blaze.

It was now in full glory, a crackling, hissing monster, flames like orange devil fingers, smoke like daylight ghosts escaping into the sky. We stood near enough to be kissed by its heat; the day was hot enough already, and sweat beaded our brows. We didn't speak, no words were necessary. Then, when the fire was at its height, at some unspoken signal, we turned away and fetched our bikes.

Andy had a metallic green Grifter, a frivolous machine with ridiculously high handlebars, whilst I had a Raleigh 5-speed racer, orange and blue, a proper bike. I could always burn him off on it. And so it proved that day, as I selected the lowest gear pedalled, perspiring, up the winding slope of Redford Lane, enjoying the shade provided by its high hedges. Andy straggled behind, the Grifter was no match for my racer, and I waited at the junction for him to appear, red-faced and grimacing, whilst I tried not to appear too smug.

"The Rec," I said.

Andy nodded. "Yeah. The Rec," he gasped.

And so we set off down the main road towards the village, the image of our creation embedded in my mind, a blazing beacon, a scorching transgression.

The Rec was the big park in the centre of the village, so called because of the recreation ground in its centre which comprised cricket and football pitches. At one end was the large red-brick block of the new Community Centre, and at the other was the Star, the other two sides were a row of houses and the village church. At the Star end of the Rec was a playground with swings, roundabouts, a see-saw and an immense metal climbing frame. Andy and I leaned our bikes against the bottom of the frame and clambered to the top. From here we could see over the houses to the main road which led to Redford Lane. The blue horizon was disappointingly clear.

"Burned itself out," muttered Andy.

I made no comment. In my mind I could see our fire raging and raging then sinking into a pile of ash, emitting a last plume of smoke and, concrete beneath it and nothing else to ignite, dying down to a few glowing embers.

"We could always see if it's on the news later," said Andy. That was a big part of it – seeing if our work would be reported in the news. So far it had not been, and as there had been no witnesses, as far as we knew, to our latest effort, there wouldn't be tonight.

A sudden gust of wind dried the sweat on my forehead, moved coolly through my hair. "We'll have to try again."

"How? That was our last one."

I began to climb down.

"That was our last one, we'll have to stop now," repeated Andy as he picked up his bike and began to wheel it across the Rec. I could hear relief in his voice and it made me angry.

"No way. We'll just have to get another box. Or a lighter. Your mum smokes. Nick hers."

"No way! Yours smokes too. And your dad. That pipe! You nick one!"

We bickered in this way as we wheeled our bikes across the sun-bleached grass in the direction of the Community Centre. The obvious thing would have been to buy some matches, but we were both only ten, and Jack the news-agent knew us and our parents, so it was too big a risk. We had to resort to finding or stealing. The box we had just used up I had found on the wall of the Star car park. I'd just pocketed it without thinking. There had only been about a dozen matches in it, but that was enough to start us off. It was the summer holidays, six weeks that seemed like an eternity to us back then. We'd set a total of eight fires so far, firstly in muddy lanes out of sight of prying eyes, well away from houses and people – we didn't want to hurt anybody or damage property. We had got bolder and bolder and lately had started setting fires 'in the open' like this last one on the concrete hardstanding outside the sewage works. We, or rather I, had plans for future conflagrations, but it looked like it was all over now.

We parted company outside the Community Centre, Andy wobbling off on his Grifter whilst I took the long way round the streets to my house, home in time for tea, and the news, which I watched half-expectantly, but was of course disappointed.

That wasn't the end of it.

A week or so later, after parking my bike in the garage,

I had a little mooch round as I sometimes did, looking through the assorted tools and junk to see if I could find anything interesting or useful. It was amazing, some of the stuff Dad kept in there. A mangle, in which Andy and I used to execute worms and slugs. Old jazzmags, until Mum made him chuck them out. Pre-decimal coins, which I spirited away and hid in my room, in the hope they might be valuable in the future. And this time, as if ordained by destiny, an old cigarette lighter. It was one of Mum's, a metallic blue Swan Vesta model bearing the image of a golden swan, the finish chipped and worn, showing the silver metal underneath. I wiped off the dust and cobwebs and polished it until the metallic blue glinted in the dim light of the garage. Expecting nothing, I flicked the sparkwheel, creating a spark which cast mad shadows up and down the brick walls, and indeed got nothing, the first time. But on the second try, the lighter sustained a flame – a tiny bud, quivering and tremulous, but a flame, nonetheless.

It was enough.

Time to go up a level.

The Industrial Estate was at the opposite end of the village to the sewage works, and it had a similar allure, perhaps even a greater attraction. Completely sealed off behind a mighty (to us) chain-link fence topped with three forbidding strands of silver barbed wire, it consisted of a series of massive warehouses and a red-brick office complex. Artics would enter and leave the place all day and into the night. It was only, we found out as we grew up and discovered the mundane realties of the adult world, a distribution centre for supermarkets, but to us, it was everything from a secret Government UFO base to the lair of a Bond villain.

It had always been in my mind as a target for our campaign, and now I had the Swan lighter, there was no stopping us.

Andy, however, took a lot of convincing. I'd seen it in his eyes at the sewage works fire and on the climbing frame, a hesitancy bordering on fear, fear that he'd gotten in over his head, that it was getting too much. But I talked him round, as his fascination with fire, the thrill of setting, of watching the flames grow and consume, was, at that point, greater than this fear.

And so one Saturday afternoon we set off on a bike ride out to the next village (at least that's what we told everyone) but instead of zooming down the curving hill and heading off west, we stopped at the bottom of the hill, braking sharply – Andy's brakes squealing alarmingly – and instead doubled back east, into the lane which ran along the south of the village, and which abutted, about half-way along, the rear of the Industrial Estate.

This lane, Back Lane, was completely unrideable, even in a dry hot summer like this one. It was narrow, bordered on the right by a thick hedge, and on the left by a steep slope. In winter it was a quagmire, and in summer a stumbly ankle-snapping obstacle course, almost completely overgrown. We couldn't even push our bikes along it, so we left them hidden near the entrance, and forced our way along the sweltering green tunnel, sweating and sneezing and falling into each other.

After a while we came to the place I had in mind, an area where a gap had been forced through the vegetation on the slope. We crawled through this, dirtying the knees of our jeans, and emerged into a narrow strip of dusty mud at the top of the slope. This formed a sort of foot-wide ledge, on the far side of which ran the formidable chain-link fence, beyond which we could see the blocky buildings of the Industrial Estate.

Panting, sweating, we crouched there for a moment, peering through the diamond pattern of the fence. No-one was about, everyone was presumably inside, busy working on their schemes of world domination. Wordlessly, we began to assemble our pyre, gathering dried grass, sticks and other detritus and shoving them into a pile, taking care not to pack it loosely, to allow air to circulate to feed the flames. To this, we added some old newspapers we'd brought in Andy's rucksack, tearing up the pages and crumpling them into balls. Pretty soon we had an acceptable pyre; not as big as the sewage works job, but it would suffice. Someone in the Industrial Estate was bound to see it! We were certain to make the news.

I slid the lighter out from my jeans pocket. Its tarnished metal gleamed enticingly. Andy shuffled back along the ledge on his knees. I sparked the lighter, and lo, it lit the first time. Shielding the minuscule flame with one hand, I leaned towards the pyre, holding my breath, introducing the tiny bud to one of the bunched-up balls of newspaper.

"HOY! What you two tykes up to!"

As if out of nowhere, a security guard loomed just beyond the fence, his uniformed figure a black shadow come to life.

I dropped the lighter. The flame went out. Andy bolted down the slope, crashing through the dense greenery. I picked up the lighter, leapt to my feet. I was choking with terror and excitement. My mouth was set in a rictus grin. I couldn't move.

"Gertcha, ya little sod!" roared the security guard. A booted foot kicked the fence. The sudden metallic rattle spurred me to action and I half-tumbled down the slope, the lighter gripped in my sweaty hand. I legged it back along Back Lane. I felt thwarted, but also elated. I hadn't set a fire but the encounter with the guard had set one within me. I risked a glance behind as I ran. Was he following? Had he called his colleagues? Had he called the police? This was, despite the lack of conflagration, surely going to make the news!

I caught up with Andy as he was extricating his bike from its hiding place. I retrieved mine.

"The George?" said Andy breathlessly.

It was a good idea. "The George."

We mounted our bikes and pedalled off out of the village, following the route we'd told everybody we'd be taking that morning.

The George was a den situated a mile or so out of the village. It was a big old tree in the middle of a copse next to a small pool. This tree, I can't remember what it was, had an unusually low, thick branch, sprouting four feet from the ground and running almost parallel to it. It was this branch that had been dubbed, by children of some previous generation, the George, but the reason was lost to time.

Andy and I sat on the branch, our legs dangling free, our bikes propped against the trunk. Andy panted, face pale, eyes nervous.

"We've been out to Doynton and on our way back we've stopped here for a rest."

Andy said nothing.

"Andy! Repeat what I say. We have to get our stories straight. Where have we just been?"

"Doynton," he mumbled. He glanced at me and I knew in that instant that I had lost him, that the fear had taken him over. "Then stopped here for a rest."

"Excellent. Whatever anyone says, whoever asks, stick to that."

Andy looked away. I could see his Adam's apple going. Was he crying?

I slid the lighter from my pocket. Already I was itching to go again. But where? Not here – the George was sacred.

Time to go up another level, to the top level. Bailey's Field.

I held the lighter out to Andy, like a talisman. "Hey, Andy, you know Farmer Bailey," I began, but I was prevented from continuing as Andy savagely swiped the lighter from my hand and before I could react had thrown it into the pool. It vanished with a plop. I watched the ripples radiate out across the dark surface of the water.

A strange calmness descended over me. I knew now I was alone. "You shouldn't have done that."

"Oh sod off!" cried Andy, shoving me so I almost fell off the George, himself sliding off it to stand, hands on hips, glaring up at me. "You're a nutter, you know that? One day you're gonna kill someone, or yourself!"

I jumped down to face him. "Don't be so stupid, we always take care!"

"'We?'" He was sobbing now, snot dribbling from his nose. It was pathetic. "There is no 'we' anymore." He picked up his bike, keeping an eye on me. "There's something wrong with you. You're damaged, weirdo. I always thought it, now I know. You're a spaz!"

And with that he was gone, wobbling back towards the village on his metallic green Grifter.

I watched him go with no emotion. I didn't need him. It was better on my own. Less chance of being caught. Bailey's Field would be mine alone.

I picked up my bike and set off in the opposite direction to Andy, taking the long way home, giving myself time to think. I couldn't guarantee that Andy wouldn't tell on me, so I had to make my next move soon.

I might not need Andy – but with the lighter gone, I needed a new source. There was nothing for it – I had to brazen it out with Jack.

It was surprisingly easy. I let a few days pass first, in case the aftermath of the Industrial Estate caught up with me. It didn't, and there was, as usual, nothing on the news about my escapades. So the next Wednesday morning I cycled to the 'precinct' – a square in the middle of the village with a supermarket, a hairdresser and a newsagents – propped my bike up against the glass window and strolled into Jack's.

Jack was tall, bald, bespectacled and avuncular, but don't let his friendly demeanour fool you – with shoplifters and any sort of troublemaker, he was brutal. Rumour was he'd used to work in a London pub like the ones off the telly. Also that he kept a sawn-off shotgun behind the counter. Both certainly untrue, but we were boys – we read a lot of comics and watched a lot of telly.

So I walked right up to the counter, plonked some coins down atop the newspapers displayed there and said, as airily as I could manage, "Box of matches, please, Jack?"

"Swan Vesta or England's Glory?"

The immediacy of his reply stalled me. "Er… England's Glory. They – it's me mum, her lighter's knackered."

Without comment, Jack retrieved the little box of matches and placed it next to my coins. I reached for it but before I could pick it up, he placed a thin, twig-like finger on it, trapping it. He leaned forwards so his old brown eyes, steady and wide behind his glasses, stared right into my very soul.

"They are for your mum, aren't they, lad?" His voice was gravelly yet soft, his tone that of a Detective Inspector interrogating a dodgy suspect.

"Yeah! Course!" I said, indignantly.

Jack nodded slowly, straightened up and took my money. It was the exact money, I knew how much such things cost.

And then I was biking back home, a new box – a new, complete, box, average contents 75 – in my jeans pocket.

So Bailey's Field was to be my next target. The village was surrounded by farms, some diary, some cereal crops. The nearest was Farmer Bailey, who was proud of his barley, which he planted in the winter to harvest in spring, and a summer crop to harvest in autumn. This latter was now almost fully-grown, a vast expanse of straw-coloured stalks undulating to the horizon, providing a sharp contrast with the blue sheet of the sky.

It had been a hot, dry summer. The barley would go up a treat, and the whole of Bailey's Field would burn, filling the sky with beautiful billows of jet-black smoke. No two ways about it, that was bound to get on the news!

And no-one would know it was me.

I returned home, parking my bike in the garage as usual, going over the plan in my mind. There were still two weeks of school holiday left. I was pretty certain Andy hadn't blabbed, so I had plenty of time. Probably safe to leave it a week, to make sure. I could then enjoy looking forward to it, the culmination of my plans.

When I went into the house, the phone in the kitchen was ringing, and, light of heart, I picked up the receiver. "Abson 3433," I trilled, in imitation of Mum.

"Hello, young chap, is your mother there?"

I went cold all over. That voice was unmistakable. "Er, yeah, Jack, I'll just go and get her."

Mum was sitting in the lounge reading The Sun and smoking. "Who is it?" she said, without looking up from her paper, or saying hello to me.

I considered lying. What was the use? "Jack."

"What the hell does he want?" Mum muttered. She balanced her fag on the rim of the ashtray and heaved herself off the settee.

I hung about as she walked through the kitchen to the phone in the dining-room. I was done for, I knew it. I took out the box of matches, stared at it. Perhaps I should hide it, throw it away? But I couldn't. I couldn't bear to part with the opportunities it presented.

Footsteps. I shoved the box back into my pocket, wincing at the tiny but distinctive rattling sound it made.

Mum slumped back down on the settee, frowning and muttering.

"What did Jack want?" I asked as innocently as possible.

"Eh?" Mum's fag had gone out and she lit it again. She glared at me suspiciously, the orange end glowing, reminding me forcefully of my achievements. "Why d'you wanna know?"

I shrugged. "Just curious."

Mum mumbled something about the price of their

newspaper delivery going up, and I sloped off to my room, greatly relieved.

My room was my sanctuary, my library, my base of command. It contained all my childhood toys (the early ones carefully boxed away), my books and comics, my old coins, and my notes and plans – in code, of course. I took out the folder for Bailey's Field and spread the contents out over the horrible flowery counterpane of my bed. I looked over the map, going over the escape routes, the point of ignition, potential hazards. Satisfied, I took the England's Glory from my jeans, and slid open the little cardboard drawer. The sight of those 75 (approx) soldiers standing to attention, all clean and neat, their white wooden stalks and bright pink heads so full of potential, excited me. Each one of them had the power to destroy, yet the power to create something beautiful. And that power was quite literally in my hand. I felt like Caesar Nero.

Unable to resist, I tickled a match out from the rank and file and struck it. It hissed and roared into life, the newborn flame dancing madly yet briefly, then settling down to the steady orange burn I knew so well.

I gazed at it, giving myself to it, thinking of Bailey's Field ablaze, of watching the news –

The flame spluttered and a blob of burning sulphur plopped down onto my bed. The counterpane, a horrible flowery yellow thing that Mum insisted on keeping over the sheets when not in use 'to keep them clean', was made of some sort of nasty foam material and it caught immediately. The material curled and melted and a flame flower blossomed. I leapt up, staring, still half-hypnotised, as the flame spread, excitingly, horribly quickly. The smell of burning plastic made me gag. Only when the conflagration reached my plans did I act. I ran from my room, down the stairs and into the kitchen. I opened the door to the cupboard under the sink, dragged out a bucket and began to fill it. I was shaking, my mind torn asunder: I didn't want to kill this beautiful new fire – but I didn't want it to consume my sanctuary – so it had to die.

"What's that smell?" Mum bustled into the kitchen. She saw what I was doing and gaped. "What are you doing?"

"Nothing!" I managed to gasp, and heaved the slopping bucket out of the sink and headed for the stairs.

Mum's voice went up an octave. "What's going on?"

I ran up the stairs, bucket banging against my knees, water slopping onto the carpet. Mum was right behind me. The air was rank with the smell of burning foam. I staggered into my bedroom, and a wall of heat hit my face

The entire bed blazed, a roaring monster, flames buffeting the ceiling. Evil black smoke roiled everywhere. I threw the water, there was a harsh sizzle and a cloud of white steam. It had no effect.

Behind me, Mum screamed.

I threw the bucket into the flames and ran back out of my room. Mum and I almost fell down the stairs. Tears streamed down my face. I don't recall much of what happened next. I remember standing outside, looking up at my room, the window black with smoke. I remember

Mum yelling over the fence to next door, "Norma! Call 999!" I remember the fire engines coming, two of them, and the firemen running into the house.

But most of all I remember Mum's face, her expression a mixture of anger and fear, her eyes regarding me as if she didn't recognise me. "What have you done?" she kept saying over and over again. "Just wait till your father gets home. What have you done?"

And yes, this particular fire *did* make the news.

After that, it all came out. Jack told Mum I had bought the matches. Andy grassed, blabbed, spilt the beans, telling everything. I confessed, what choice did I have? There was a lot of fuss. Dad shouted at me and my pocket money was stopped. The police were called in, but as I was too young, no charges were pressed. I had to go and see a special doctor, who asked me lots and lots of questions and who seemed to understand why I did what I did. He even gave it a special name, 'pyromania.' Andy was right – there was something wrong with me – but I wasn't a spaz – I was a pyromaniac.

So that was that. All out in the open. And my sanctuary destroyed – all my books and comics, and plans (though that was probably a good thing, considering). The only things that has survived were those dratted coins I'd filched from the garage. The worst of it was, the knowledge that I could have died in the fire. Could have killed Mum, and Dad if he'd been off work. Could have killed the entire street. I couldn't stop thinking about it. Such power. From such a little thing.

Weeks passed. The summer holidays ended. I went back to school. I saw Andy again, though he refused to speak to me or even look at me. My room got completely redecorated, and I began to fill it with books and comics again, replacing valued or cherished items where I could. Mum and Dad remained watchful, but I did my best to be a good boy. A reformed offender. My pocket money started again. I put it to good use.

Although it was now September, the days were still hot. An Indian summer was upon us.

Saturday, and I was out on my bike as usual. I'd been over to Doynton, for real this time, and on the way back stopped off at the George. I sat on the branch for a while, thinking. Then I set off again, back out of the village. It was a balmy, hot day, just past midday, and the sun was high in the cloudless sky.

Perfect.

I propped my bike against the south gate to Bailey's Field, climbed over the stile and set off into the rustling ranks of barley, reaching into my jeans pocket for the magnifying glass that nestled snugly there.

We Are Where We Are

By Kevin MacCabe

When Leo opened his eyes there was something different about the sitting room. It was filled with smoke. It shouldn't have been a complete surprise as he had smelt smoke earlier in the day, but a cursory inspection had not disclosed its source, so he had decided to watch the football. Tedious defensive play from both sides had sent the game to a dreary nil-nil and him to sleep. In the meantime the situation in his house had apparently deteriorated and ignoring it was clearly no longer an option.

He rolled off the sofa onto the floor knocking over a half-filled can of lager, which was annoying, now he would have to clean the carpet as well. Better stay low, that seemed to be the thing to do, he had seen it in a film or something, and so he crawled over to the door. Fumes were streaming up from the basement utility room but the hall was otherwise clear so he stood up and went to the kitchen to get a bucket of water. He had a fire extinguisher under the stairs, but it was new and rather expensive. Better to wait for a real emergency.

After a brief search, he remembered his bucket was catching a drip at the back of the toilet in the bathroom, so he went up the one and a half flights of the quirky three storey building to get it. The bath taps thundered a good twenty litres of water into the bucket and he took it to tackle the orange flame that was now licking along the skirting boards in the hall. The liquid load arrested its progress and he returned upstairs for a refill.

When he tried to descend again, the bottom step was glowing a healthy red, so he tipped the water over the bannister. It hissed and fizzled but did not make much of an impression. The lower storey looked lost.

We are where we are, he thought. As long as the fire stayed where it was, he would be ok, so he went in to the bedroom to think about what to do next.

The afternoon sun poured in as he opened the curtains. Across the road he could see another house also on fire. In the window of the second floor his neighbour was sitting in his study watching television which he found reassuring. In his own house, he realised the kitchen was now out of commission, but he didn't really need a kitchen to live, he thought, he could order takeaways. His plan to adapt to life one and a half floors up began to take shape.

No 'fridge, was a bit of an issue, but when he was a student he had made one using a bucket of water and a large cloth. It was good enough for six packs of beer, so it would probably do for milk and cheese.

The master bedroom would serve as his new living

room and from now on he could sleep in the spare room, although he would have to move some of those boxes. In fact, he could throw them down the stairs and the fire would burn them.

Okay, this was better, these were solutions.

He moved the double bed over to allow room to set up an office. He would have to work from home now that he couldn't get out. See, it wasn't all bad.

All the running around had made him feel sleepy. He assumed that was what it was, although the smoke made him a bit drowsy too. So he decided to take a nap. His acceptance that he had to move on from living at street level had taken all the stress out of the situation and he slept very well.

When he awoke it was dark. He found a can of lager under the bed, it was his lucky day, and cracked it open. Looking across the road, he could see his neighbour still slumped in front of his television. He raised the can in his direction, sound bloke, he wasn't panicking, took a swig and went to the bathroom.

He stumbled to the toilet across the landing, now dense and black with smoke. When he flushed he realised he had no soap, so he wrote it down. There were bound to be lots of things he would need for his new elevated lifestyle.

Outside the bathroom, tongues of flame lapped at the top of the stairs and the carpet was smouldering. The fire was advancing faster than expected, which was a big disappointment. He had been thinking that the ground floor fire was really a problem he could leave for the next owner. Well, he had a third floor; that was the advantage of these townhouses, what a shrewd purchase. So he gathered a pillow and his toothbrush and made his way upstairs again.

If the fire spread any further, he always had the attic. And, if he was honest, it could do with a clear out.

Four Poems

By Kimberly Nugent

mathematics of fire
increasing complexity in melting wax
fluidity of flame

nourished by dried tinder
promethean spark
consumes the forest nursemaid

dense atmosphere of titan
was pierced by the eagle at the rock
revealing the ancient's flame and thunder
while the secrets of plasma propulsion
are stolen from Jupiter's feet

the smouldering singularity
a point on the horizon
consuming both life and death
spreads horizontally
ash sealing the firmament

*He who cannot light a fire knows
nothing about love.*

~ FINNISH PROVERB

The Comfort of Public Fireplaces

BY B. ANNE ADRIAENS

The Old Mill rises from the surrounding water meadows, centuries-old foundations dipped in river silt. Visited upon by every kind of weather, witness to the changes caused by an increasing human presence, it felt the ground shudder as ancient woodlands were felled and ever more machines were used for transport, for farming, for construction, slowly chewing at the landscape. And it, too, changed.

More of an inn than a mill these days, people come here looking for company, swapping stories and gossip, away from those things that became a burden through an excess of familiarity. Hours pass, hardly noticed, food and drink is bought and consumed — the place is kept lively. But the Old Mill doesn't care about the people; its sole concern is the centre of the downstairs room, the fire in the grate, its beating heart.

Those who cross the threshold rarely do more than

cast a glance at the flames, part of that quick survey of the room before they settle down. Though had the fire not been there, they would've felt something was missing. The kind of something one cannot put one's finger on. Perhaps because of the chill that creeps up from the floor when the fire goes out, making the air within the brick and flint walls shiver. The ghost of woodlands past is quick to claim what once belonged to it, no matter how long ago.

One late afternoon, when the place is brimming with chatter and laughter, a young woman catches the mill's attention. She's sitting at the small round table in front of the grate, only half-listening to her companion. Her gaze keeps darting back to the struggling flames and, slowly, a thin line appears between her eyebrows. *It's going to die*, she says. To which he replies, *just leave it…* But she hears the reproach between the lines, decides it doesn't matter if others find her odd and gets up. Kneeling on the cold stones, she grabs the iron poker and starts stirring the embers.

She behaves as though a dream has caught hold of her – until the barman drops an armload of logs on the blue stone ledge. He's grinning, amused that a customer would bother with the fireplace, let alone manage to get it going. A bit surprised too. He turns it into a joke – the friendly sort. And he'll never know about the kids some thirty years ago who had worn rather different grins when they teased her about matches and lighters and other things, back when she wouldn't go near any kind of flame and shied away from putting a Christmassy cheer in the classroom. Before he leaves, she tells him that she misses the open fire at her old house, adds in a whisper: *apart from my cat, it's the only thing I miss from that place.*

The air around her curls into a thousand smiles as she starts rebuilding the fire, silently addressing it, thoughts bouncing off the stones encasing the flames. She hears her companion's words tense with objection, just like when they were still a couple, his voice tinny and distant: unimportant. The story she's about to tell the house is the only thing that matters right now.

Nearly forty years earlier, many miles away across the water, a small patch of land planted with trees caught fire. It was a clear spring day and the man who owned it had decided to gather the dead leaves left by the previous autumn and burn them. But the wind picked up, scattering the smouldering remnants, ushering the flames among the trees until they found better fuel. Until their brightness and heat reached the nearest house and started licking its brick walls. Smoke slipped through a door left ajar, its panic-inducing smell preceded by a seven year old girl. Her screams shook her heavily pregnant mother from her slumber.

And so another child was born.

The night was nearing its darkest hour when she entered this world; the fire had died out and the trees were crying softly over their charred limbs. Having swallowed her mother's fears – that flame-fuelled adrenalin like a toxic cocktail – she shivered in a heated cot, waiting to be welcomed within the echoing walls she later tried to call home.

Seasons passed and the forest grew back in a harmony of greens on black, while she, no longer a baby, repeatedly dreamed of the house being on fire, and three corpses laid out under the stairs: mother, father and sister. Still bodies, burning in silence. Every night she would watch them, sitting on her haunches, arms hugging her knees. The roaring flames felt like a welcome embrace, not hurting at all but pleasant. And every morning would find her puzzled as she realised how scared she should have been.

Yet here she is, after the passing decades cleansed her of those fears that used to play tricks on her senses, until what she was left with was something close to fascination. Until her fingers learned to tame the flames, stroking the shimmering, heated air, coaxing them to grow and shine brighter. Until old dreams and childhood taunts no longer mattered.

The air within the Old Mill's walls moves slowly, every particle paying attention. And as the minutes pass one by one, it begins to slumber like an old lady who's had a long day. Yet the stones have soaked up the woman's thoughts, and they remember that fire can be both pain and bliss.

By the time she's done telling her story, her companion has left and her meal has gone cold. She looks around. The two old men who were seated at the bar have gone home. The tables with their empty plates and glasses and dirty cutlery look forlorn. Chairs are left the way they were when people got up. The friendly barman is nowhere to be seen.

Her pint of ale has gone flat but she finishes it anyway; the food she leaves for the genius loci. There's no one looking her way when she gets up, there's no one to clear her table, let alone ask where her companion's gone to. Not that she would have the answer to that, not these days, not after she chose to leave him.

The last log crumbles into charred fragments, blazing briefly before resuming a gentler smouldering. She gives the tiniest nod then puts on her scarf and coat and walks out, turns left, across the small weir and along the narrow raised path between the meadows with their sleeping sheep, watched over by the cathedral spire. The streetlights punctuating the path resemble fairy lanterns dangling in the darkness; they hint at new routes into different worlds. When she finally leaves the town, she doesn't come back.

But the Old Mill is still standing, its walls of stone,

brick and flint as strong as ever. It's still letting people in from the cold and the rain, knowing that the woman who had looked after its fire one evening was only passing through.

It's waiting. Waiting for someone who, once more, will look after its heart.

Smoke

By Pete W. Sutton

"What is it?" I had asked innocently.

"Smoke" she replied.

"Yes, but what is it!"

"It will make you fly in your dreams." That's what she said, that's what made me take it.

The users that had been on it the longest spent most of their lives asleep. It wasn't a party drug. Some took sleeping pills too. Keeping themselves out of the land of the waking.

'It will make you fly in your dreams.' How little that explains and yet how enticing it sounds. Little bags of yellow dust looking like powdered ginger. Smelling of exotic places, of dream, of wind. They said that it came from Madagascar. I didn't really care.

"Smoke, ginger, broom, zippy," they say now on street corners. Many names for a nameless high, a manikin root ground up dry and crumbled into a pipe giving sweet smoke-filled dreams. I am an eagle, a jinn, a supersonic jet.

I fly. The ground zips past beneath me. Everything is hyper real; I feel the wind on my face, the calls of surprised birds, the smell of summer clouds. I fly.

Three days later I realise that I never asked for her name or number, never noticed that she'd gone after our first, and so far only, night together. I woke with a buzz, dressed in a kinetic rush and ran for the door. I had to have more.

"Ginger, broom, zippy, pipe!"

"Yeah give me some my man, I need to fly tonight."

This was no gateway, this was all the way inside enemy country.

The inevitable phone calls "Why aren't you in work today?", "I cooked dinner for you, the least you could do was phone to say you weren't coming!", "Dude not seen you for ages, fancy a drink?" Goodbye job, family, friends, hello flight, hello smoke.

"You know when you leap from a height and fall in water?" I asked Joe, who called round one day, worried about me. "Well it's nothing like that really, but you know the buzz you get when you've survived a fall like that? The buzz I imagine skydivers feel?"

"Uh-huh."

Joe was like that, man of few words, I was already itching to get back to it, to jump off the cliff of awake and fly on wings of smoke.

"You'll just have to try it."

I was a bad friend, the first hit is always free, isn't that what pushers do? Joe was my best friend but I brought him in all the same. The waking world had ceased to hold my attention. I was vaguely apprehensive about that. Like the time I spotted that one of my moles was bleeding and did nothing about it. I was worried for a while but the feeling eventually went away. You just can't hold bad things in your mind all the time. The minutiae of life make you forget until you glance in a mirror and see that the mole is a different colour, has grown larger and is reminding you that 'something bad is going to happen.' Not that it ever did. My mole that is. It didn't get any worse. I eventually stopped worrying about it, or rather my worries got further and further apart.

Anyway the first bad sign was that the phone stopped working. I hadn't been paying the bills. I hadn't been paying any bills. All my money was going on Smoke and sleeping pills. I had lost track of time. I thought that, you know, I'd get bored of flying and get on with my life again soon. I was using more, taking more pills too. My life, as they say on those adverts, was spiralling out of control. I hadn't seen Joe again after the first couple of times he crashed at mine. I sometimes wondered where he was.

I realised I didn't know who she was, or why I listened (because I was trying to get in her pants obviously) or where she went. I have taken to looking for her in cafes and bars. Amongst the sad fuckers washed up on the streets (with that nagging sensation that I would be there soon,) in shops, next to traffic lights. It's how I spend my days, my waking hours. You can only sleep so long. That's how I caught a glance in the mirror. On the street. In a department store. I was thin, stick-like, with ravaged eyes, unwashed, matted hair. I needed to fly. My stash was running low. I would need to get more soon.

"Coke, Blow, Uppers, E," they say as I walked past. "Broom?" I say hopefully. "There ain't no smoke no more dude. The man shut it down. Was only being grown in one lab. Some genetically modified shit, a Frankendrug. There is no more. D'ya want some Acid or Shrooms, they'll make you fly."

No smoke? None to be had ever again? I went to Joe's but he wasn't there. Hadn't been for a week or so. Had been thrown out by his landlord for not paying his bills. As I said, I'm a bad friend. I wondered why he'd never come to my place. After I mean. Perhaps he was dead. Perhaps she was dead? Perhaps she was only a figment of my imagination?

I staggered home, kicked open the swollen door, put the latest red letters on the pile with the rest. I went to the bedroom. All I could smell was those high summer clouds, an exotic spice. I checked, enough for a few pipes, enough pills. Smoke and pills. I need flame to survive.

I am careful to drop the empty packets down between the floorboards where they won't find them. The brown spicy smoke swirls around the room as I lie down and close my eyes. I will fly forever now.

Memories to the Flames

By Pete W. Sutton

It felt good not to write. Eventide and all the other scriveners in their cells scribbling away. Elisenda had followed the ritual, had burned the powder, but, tonight, for the first time, hadn't inhaled. Had held her breath in fact, for as long as possible. The compulsion to write wasn't there.

The light burned overhead, the inspectoress stalked the corridors and Elisenda allowed herself a secret smile. She'd done it. It had been bubbling inside her for ages. What if she just… didn't?

And now she knew.

It was fine. She glanced out the little window set high up the door to see the inspectoress watching one of her fellow Scriveners through her own hatch. Elisenda had a little time. She didn't know how to disguise the smell if she burnt tonight's page. And besides, they'd know, a torn out sheet would be obvious.

She'd have to come up with a plan. She'd used the

powder already. She'd just have to make something up.

The link between the ritual, the powder and the words they each produced night after night wasn't obvious. The deity spoke to them and they produced automatic writing. That's what they were told. But Elisenda wondered if it was merely drug-dreams.

She could hear the inspectoress approaching. She dipped her quill, briefly wondering, as usual, what bird such a massive, night-black feather came from. To work her way within she'd need alliteration. She scribbled something, a snatch of conversation she'd overheard in the halls. Aware that the inspectoress watched. When she heard the footsteps recede she opened the book at a random place to read what she'd written before, under the influence.

And sad the sea, and dark the waves and cold the shore. And fierce the air, and deep the fall and dry the cave. And tired of wing, and hungry of belly and desirous of shelter.

She'd written nonsense. Never before had she read her drugged writing. It was strictly forbidden. Only the priests could do so. But tonight she was breaking all their rules. Tonight she had broken free of the secret flame.

When the lights flicked out and the corridors were filled with the sighs of frustrated writers denied putting more words on the page, Elisenda closed her journal with a frisson of illicit satisfaction. It felt glorious.

But now she was faced with a new problem. She couldn't sleep. Always, under the influence of the powder, she'd been straight to sleep after evening ritual. But now she was aware of the sounds of snoring coming from the other cells, the cold draft coming from her partly open window, and the regular thump of the inspectoress's patrol.

Tomorrow. She promised. Tomorrow I'll do it again. And I'll escape.

Favila paused at the bottom of the steps, as he usually did. His knees and hips hurt more tonight. Soon he'd have to find an apprentice and initiate a boy into the ways of the depths. Just as he'd been initiated so many decades ago. One already chosen to undergo the warden training, like he'd been. Each year the priests collected children from the surrounding villages to replace those that grew too old for the work. Boys to be wardens, girls to be Scriveners, a gold piece to the parents. Each year though the crop of children was less. The buildings fell into disrepair, the tasks were lessened due to fewer hands at work. They faced decline and fall. Yet, they could, for now, still command the commoners who relied upon the order for indulgences and prophecy.

He plucked the black-iron key from his belt and unwrapped the chain, giving the key a kiss before placing it in the iron-bound oak of the entrance. He mumbled a quick prayer and unlocked the door. As it swung open he raised the torch, careful to hold it away from his head. He could ill afford to lose any more hair. As ever the sound of small bells filled the air and, despite the underground darkness, there was a hint of summer light and spring flowers in the cave.

He hastened through the door and locked it behind

him.

More steps, more strain upon old hips and knees but now he gave it no thought. His heart swelled with love, and awe and pride and fear – the same old mix of emotions. Nearer, my god, to thee.

The black angel lay on the slab as if dead. Its midnight wings thrust out to each side of its curled form. Favila crossed himself and offered up a quick fragment of Psalm: "yea, he did fly upon the wings of the wind."

As he approached, the sound of softly ringing bells became omnipresent and the angel itself gave off a heady perfume. Favila drew forth the other tools of his position. The scraper and the deep-throated flask.

The angel's body glistened in the light of the torch Favila had placed in the sconce beside it. Skin black and oleaginous with ink. The walls of the cave had been filled with writing. Small and large, words over words. The day wardens would puzzle over it tomorrow, as they did every day. But Favila's task was easier. Or harder. He didn't know. He bent to it now and chose the angel's left arm, raising it delicately – even though the angel had never, in all the many decades he'd tended to it, awoken. Like a man in form but vastly larger, some fourteen feet from the tips of its toes to the crown of its head. And the wings – the massive, jet wings – they would stretch from one wall of its cell to the other.

Yes, he thought of it as a cell. Although that was blasphemous. The priest who'd taught him as a boy, carrying the deep-throated flask in awe, had spoken about how the order protected the celestial being from the jealous.

From those who wished ill upon them. The order who kept themselves apart from the rest of the population of Newland. The declining order.

But Favila knew they kept the angel here as much to keep it for themselves, as to protect it. Although it hadn't awakened for many decades, more than Favila had been alive, the writings were very clear that when it did wake it wanted to fly. Any creature with such wings would want to fly.

He started at the fingertips and scraped the unctuous black substance into the flask. Later he'd mix it with bergamot and pine resin, frankincense and camphor as well as many other, secret, substances. Burning the angel's secretions formed the ritual of the dreamers. His was a sacred task, a necessary one, for the order.

Once the flask was full he pulled his notebook from the pocket of his robe and using a piece of charcoal he drew the arm and where he'd stopped. Scraping shouldn't be too deep, the ritual depended on a steady dose. Each part of it had been developed over many years by the originators of the order.

Favila's role was as prescribed as any of the others. The day wardens who studied for ten years in order to decipher the angel's writings, formed upon the walls using the angel's own blood and feathers as ink and quill. The dreaming maidens, the Scriveners, who breathed the angel's fire. The inspectoresses, who'd once been maidens themselves, but who had become immune to the powder over a period of many years. Not all became immune. Some slipped ever further into dreaming, until all they did was sleep and write until they starved.

Once he'd noted the exact position of the scraping, he returned the notebook to its pocket and hung the scraper back on his belt. He grabbed the flask with his left hand and lifted the torch with his right. He turned and bowed to the angel and as he straightened, the angel's eye regarded him calmly. He dropped the torch. Its voice boomed. He didn't know its language, he hadn't the facility. As a child he'd failed that test and been chosen as apprentice to the Collector.

He placed the flask on the floor and retrieved the torch his mind racing, his heart booming, his muscles trembling. Awe, and fear and flight. The angel had raised itself on an elbow and gazed at him unblinking. He bowed again, mind gabbling, and backed away. The angel asked him a question, but again his mind could not encompass its language. Not many could. He could feel the bounds of his sanity being blown in the gale of its thoughts. Other men had gone mad when confronted by the angel, he knew. He turned and fled; making sure to lock the door behind him. But now he'd seen the angel awake he wondered how it could ever have fit through such a tiny door. Or how a door, no matter how thick the wood and iron, could hold it. Just before he fled up the stairs, the room behind the door flooded with light as the angel's fire erupted.

Elisenda woke to the sound of running feet and slamming doors. This burst of activity was unlike any other awakening she'd had here. She glanced at her open notebook. Open to a blank page. She'd been found out. That must be why the inspectoresses were running. They were about to burst in and drag her away to be punished. She looked around her small cell, searching for a way out, even though she knew there wasn't one.

The door burst open and she dropped to her knees and bowed her head. "Forgive me, Auntie," she said. When there was no response she looked up and Constance grinned at her. "Why, what have you done?" her friend asked.

"Connie! What's going on?" She leapt to her feet, penance temporarily forgotten.

"No idea. The Aunties have all run off!" Connie was positively hopping from one foot to another. Right now they should be standing, head bowed, awaiting the Senior Scrivener to lead them to the feast hall to breakfast. "Come on!" Connie ducked back outside and Elisenda followed. The Scriveners loitered outside their cells. Sofia, the senior, stood wringing her hands. When she saw Elisenda, the last to arrive, she drew a breath and became calm, or pretended to.

"We shall proceed to breakfast," she said, as if it were a normal day.

The girls, glancing at one another, unspoken questions brimming, formed up as they would on any other day. From tallest to shortest and oldest to youngest they formed two lines and followed Sofia to the breakfast room. They encountered no inspectoresses in the short walk down the plain white-walled corridors, their feet slapping against the darkly polished wooden floor. The smell of breakfast marched them onwards. At least the servants hadn't absconded.

After breakfast they were supposed to attend to their assigned roles. Some of the girls gardened, others did laundry, yet others worked in the library. But there were no governesses to watch over them and ensure they did the work. And yet the majority of the Scriveners went where they were supposed to go anyway. A few stayed in the breakfast hall and a couple snuck outside, separate to the gardeners, just to run free for once. Elisenda went to the library. She wasn't supposed to, had never been assigned library duty in fact, but wanted to read the others' books and this might be her best chance.

The other girls in the library watched her curiously as she wandered down the narrow aisles. There was a sweet smell of old paper, dust and the polish they used on the dark wooden bookcases. The light in the library was also the best in the house – a dome of glass acted as ceiling.

Soon the conscientious girls were absorbed in their bookbinding and indexing and Elisenda was free to roam without scrutiny. She climbed a ladder to the upper tier, grabbed a couple of books at random and, retreating to an alcove, out of sight of those below, settled down and read.

Most of the books she flicked through were filled with the same stream of unconsciousness as hers but the occasional stark passage of unintelligibility stood out. In one book it stood out because someone had drawn a red box around it. She searched and found more.

In each case where a red box had been used the language was that of the angels. Elisenda couldn't read it but Constance could! She had to know what it said – but could she trust Constance? And where was her friend anyway?

Favila, the old priest and the head inspectoress stood in front of the ironbound door. "Will it hold?" the priest asked, a second time. The first had been at the top of the stairs and he'd seemed to accept Favila's assurances. Now, here at the bottom of the stairs, the door in front of him, unearthly fire illuminating all the gaps, he didn't look as convinced when Favila nodded.

"It is a glory this has happened during our watch, Uncle," the inspectoress said breathlessly.

"Blessed be!" the priest responded. A little less enthusiastically than Favila thought he should. But then the priest was even older than he. Perhaps he had been counting on an easy life.

"Your will, Uncle?" Favila asked.

The pause was so long Favila wondered if he'd been heard, but eventually the priest sucked his teeth. "We need all those who can speak, or read, the angel's tongue. Not just the wardens but the Scriveners you have taught to do so too." Favila gasped, eyes wide, the inspectoresses taught the dreamers the angel's tongue? "It will enter its hypomania stage and we need to work in shifts to capture what it writes." The priest paused and then made shooing gestures at the inspectoress who tutted, gathered her skirts and ran up the steps with an agility and haste Favila would not have imagined.

"And you, Guardian. You know your role when it awakes. You must ensure it cannot escape. It cannot fly." Favila nodded and sighed. He lifted the key on the chain and kissed it. The priest nodded and started up the stairs, much slower and less agile than the inspectoress.

Favila had read the journals of the first guardian and all who came after. He knew the Gathering by heart having performed it daily for decades. But the Durance? That had been ritually practised of course, but never needed for many years. He reached out with the key with a trembling hand. The tools he needed were in the room. With the angel.

The door swung open to a light almost too bright to endure. The angel burned with a pure fire, without flame. Its bull-like voice formed an enquiry and Favila knew that there was a good reason he'd never been taught its tongue. He wouldn't be swayed by whatever reasons, demands and entreaties it made when he broke its wings. He squinted through the ritual mask he'd pulled over his face until he could see the angel, a black mannequin wreathed in white flame. He closed and locked the door and took a deep breath.

"Where did you get this?" Constance kept peeking through the branches of the rhododendron, its thick waxy leaves hiding them from view. Their secret place in the garden. Elisenda put her hand on Constance's arm. "No-one can see us. You know that. It's okay, please, just look at it."

Constance sighed and sat with her knees drawn up to her chin. "You know how much trouble we'll be in if they find us? With a book? From the library?"

"They're not going to find us, Connie. Please?"

Connie bit her lip. "El…"

Elisenda opened the book to the red boxed text of angel's tongue. "Please?"

Connie looked close to tears but did glance down and a frown formed. "Angel tongue?"

"It's a Scrivener's tome."

"Oh, El. It's beautiful," Connie said with a tear spilling. "Oh, it longs to fly. Why can't it fly?"

"What's it say?" Elisenda asked desperately.

"It can't be translated, exactly, but the angel is here and we are part of its dreams and memories. This is blasphemous, El, you must return this and never reveal to anyone that you had it, or that we've read it!" Connie wiped her eyes with the back of her hand and abruptly got to all fours to crawl out of their hidey-hole. "And never speak to me again about this, you hear me Elisenda? Never!"

Elisenda watched with a frown as her friend exited the bower they'd discovered together when much younger. If it wanted to be free, if it wanted to fly then what was stopping it? She looked at the house and thought about the inspectoresses and priests, wardens and Scriveners. No, not *what* was stopping it, *why* were they stopping it?

The inspectorsses had returned to the halls by the time Elisenda returned to the mansion. The illicit book tucked into her apron, snuggled in a fold of her tunic. If they searched the girls it would be terrible, but they'd never done so before. She thought her face would be a beacon of guilt though and they'd know something was wrong.

As they lined up she sought out Constance and tried to meet her eyes, Constance looked away. Also looked guilty. But it seemed the inspectoresses were nervous, some paced up and down the line, others stood in a knot, whispering.

Once the girls had lined up, in the formation they would usually be taken to their rooms, in order to start the evening's ritual. The head inspectoress, an old priest and a man Elisenda had never seen before walked up the stairs. The girls hung their heads, as they'd been taught to do when a priest was present. But Elisenda tried to watch through her fringe.

The priest wore the same grey tunic they all did but with a crimson surplice where the scriveners wore aprons. The man with him, though, wore a leather tunic that had been scored as if cut with a knife and splashed with some black liquid, like ink.

The head inspectoress walked down the line and asked some of the girls to step out, including Constance. "Girls, those of you who have been chosen, follow Uncle. The rest of you are to pray tonight. There will be no ritual. Tomorrow there will be various tasks, and you will have to do the work of these chosen ones as well, as they embark on a sacred task."

Elisenda frowned. A sacred task?

"Choose one, Favila," The priest said. It seemed that was unexpected as both the head inspectoress, and the old man in leather turned to him sharply.

"Uncle?" the old man asked.

"We cannot spare any of the wardens, and you need an apprentice at this time."

The man brushed a hand through his sparse grey hair and turned to look at the girls who hadn't been chosen. "I need a strong arm, Uncle. To complete the task."

The priest's mouth twisted. "The task you failed, Guardian."

The old man sighed, and nodded reluctantly.

"Who is the strongest?" he asked

"I am." Elisenda took a step forward lifting her head. From the corners of her eyes she saw some of the girls exchanging looks.

"You? But you're a mere slip. Surely one of the older girls—"

Elisenda repeated, "I am!" and scowled at the other girls. None gainsaid her. None wanted to be singled out.

The old man smoothed his moustache. "Very well. I can only use the tools I am provided. Follow me."

The girls who'd been chosen followed the priest, the old man followed the girls and Elisenda followed the old man. They proceeded downstairs and the priest went down the passageway towards the library but the old man carried on towards the kitchens. Elisenda caught Constance throw a backwards glance before they were out of sight around the corner.

Instead of the kitchens the old man stopped at a door

Elisenda had not paid much attention to in the past. It went to a storeroom, she thought. The old man pulled out a bunch of keys, unlocked the door, painted white, the same colour as the corridor walls. He gestured for Elisenda to precede him into the darkened alcove the door opened onto. She walked past him and squinted, trying to penetrate the gloom. The old man stepped inside, closed the door and there was a scraping sound and a torch burst into life. Ahead, past walls full of shelves holding various household equipment, lay stairs. Going down.

"Why do you need someone strong?" Elisenda asked.

"For the Durance," Favila said stepping past her and starting down the wooden stairs.

"What's a durance?" she asked following him. They quickly reached a landing and a switchback and then they started down stone steps. As they progressed deeper the stone became rougher, less worked.

"Not 'a,' 'the.' It's a ceremonial task. You'll need to hold its wing."

Could she hear bells?

"What wing?"

As they turned a last corner she saw a thickly bound oaken door set into a blank wall. The door's gaps were highlighted in a cold white light, something bright, behind the door. She could definitely hear bells, and there was a perfume she could smell even above the acrid smoke of the torch.

The old man glanced back at her. "The angel's wing."

The angel was perfect in a way she would never be able to describe. In proportion, in feature and form. Even if it hadn't been chained to the stout wooden table bolted to the floor. It half-opened its wings as they entered and white flame ran up and down its limbs and body. The sound of bells became all she could hear before it opened its mouth and bellowed words she could not decipher.

"Why's it chained?" she asked. She stared at the silver lettering running along the chain links. Spells to hold it fast. To keep it bound.

"It has always been thus," Favila answered.

Which, she noted, wasn't a proper answer.

The Guardian strode over to a cabinet against the wall. "You have to hold its wings," he said, his back to her.

"Why?"

Favila turned around and her eyes were drawn to the rusty iron sledge hammer in his hands.

"Weren't you taught to obey your elders without question, child?"

"What are you going to do with that?"

"Get over there and hold its wing. This is in the rituals. The Durance is required when it is awake. It heals when it sleeps."

Elisenda shook her head. It wanted to fly.

"If you do not I will find another who will and you will be punished."

She shook her head again and ran over to put herself between it and the man who wanted to harm it. She spread her arms. "Don't hurt it!"

Favila frowned and took a step forward, dropping the

hammer into one hand and holding the other out. He moved towards the angel. She couldn't let him and jumped in front of him. He opened his mouth to say something but she tripped him and he jerked forward. He threw the hammer up in reaction, it hit the table with a resounding smash. The angel crouched and pulled the chain as the table leg the hammer hit popped out of its metal clasp that held it to the floor.

The angel walked free, but held the long black iron chain that had secured it. Favila recovered from his stumble, Elisenda noted the look of horror on his face seconds before the chain whipped out and smashed his head like a pumpkin.

She dropped to her knees and held her hands over her face. She could hear the angel moving about. Then a clank as the chain hit the floor. The angel said something in its booming voice and she peeked through her fingers. It held up the keyring and asked a question again. She didn't need to know how to speak angel to know what it was asking. With a trembling finger she pointed to the black iron key that would unlock the door. But the door was obviously too small for the angel to fit through. The angel spoke a single word and the white fire in its fist glowed blue and the keychain and all the keys glowed red then ran through its fingers like honey.

It took a step and crouched next to her and put two fingers on her head. It felt like she stood beneath a waterfall or had fallen backwards off a cliff as her consciousness fled. The last thing she saw, down tunnel vision, as the tunnel got longer and the visible part got smaller, was the angel fully consumed in white fire, then it sprang upwards from the crouch as a column of flame blasted away the ceiling and the tons of earth above them.

Elisenda awoke to darkness and the smell of fire. She panicked until she could see that above her was slightly less dark. She crawled over to the guardian and the pile of slag that had once been keys. It had happened then. Above, as if someone had whipped away a blanket over the sky, stars suddenly blazed.

She could see, after a fashion, that the door remained locked. It felt warm and the smell of smoke grew stronger.

There was only one way out. The angel's passage had scored a roughly circular hole from the small room beneath the mansion and through the earth which steamed and smoked slightly from its passage. There were rocks and tree roots that she could use. Elisenda climbed.

As she got closer to the top she could discern a red glow and hear the whooshing sound of fire. As she crested the lip of the hole the angel had made she saw the entire mansion in flames. Knots of scared Scriveners and wardens watched as it burned. Inspectoresses wailed and priests stood stunned.

She saw Constance and ran to her friend who hugged her fiercely.

"You look terrible," Constance said.

Elisenda looked down. Her clothes were filthy and her hands were black from the soil. She shrugged.

She tried to say something and only angel tongue came out. Constance's eyes grew round. Her mind had been touched. She could feel the secret fire spark within. She was glad her friend could understand her, that Elisenda could tell her that it only wanted to fly.

She looked up to see the new star ascending.

Trace

By Amanda Staples

This was his last day as Ralf Armitage. He'd had a good life – depending on your interpretation of 'good'.

He looked at his watch then checked the time on his phone, just to be sure. No signal. Again. He'd give it a minute.

Ralf, as he was currently known, jabbed at the fire with a poker. Any document containing his name would soon be a pile of ash. RIP Ralph Armitage. He chucked on his passport. The last link. He watched a corner catch light.

His phone beeped.

He opened the message, read it, replied.

Message not sent.

Still no signal.

Ralf moved to the window, waved his phone above his head, straining to see. No bars.

He hated this place and its patchy signal. He cursed so loudly and dragged a chair to stand on across the flagstone floor so heavily he failed to hear the log crack. His back turned, Ralph failed to see the kindling drop, the passport shift; his face, partly melted, tumble onto the hearth.

Finally getting a signal, Ralf sent his acknowledgement text and left without a backward glance.

Outside, Gary Black, as his new passport detailed him, let his shoulders sag in relief. He strolled the casual walk of a free man, tossing his untrackable flip-phone in the first bin he passed. No more jobs to carry out. Ever again. He'd almost miss it. He'd been bloody good at it. Never left a trace.

Tell Me Beautiful Lies

By Chrissey Harrison

Petrol laps from the five-gallon can in my hands. There's an energy to the way it moves, quick, anxious. A pent-up need to release its potential. To release *her*.

Each glug soaks in. Trickles down between the fibres of the worn carpet. Fills the pores of the brick fireplace. Drips from the bottom hem of the curtains. Slides off the polished wood of the bureau. Swells the pages of books on the bookcase.

I love the smell of it. Sweet but tainted, heady but nauseating, pleasant but unnerving. A beautiful lie.

A splash lands on the coffee table and I watch the liquid spread over the glass until it lies almost too thin to see. The light from the setting sun slants across the table highlighting a writhing pattern of rainbow whorls, and there's a shimmer to the air from the fumes. So beautiful.

I can show you brighter patterns, she whispers. A delicious shiver passes through me. My lighter – a vintage Zippo engraved with my initials – grows heavy in my pocket and I slip my hand in to touch the metal. Warm. Alive. It was a gift from my first lover and now it is my connection to my mistress.

This house is my gift to her. The latest of many. But the last time was too close, and weeks have gone by since I indulged her.

I was rushing, too impatient for my mistress's pleasure. A footprint by the garden gate. A drop of blood on the paving slab by the back door after I caught my finger on broken window glass. A receipt, dropped from my pocket when I took the lighter out. Tiny mistakes. But the authorities look very intently at every detail when they want to stop someone as much as they want to stop *us*.

We had to lay low for a while, but we grew restless.

To tide us over, I stole a car, drove it to the derelict end of the wharf, where there's no cameras, and let her devour it. The metal groaned and buckled, paint blistered, tyres burst. She boiled from the shattered windows, white at the core, yellow and red where she reached skyward, with bursts of green, magenta, indigo, as different materials ignited.

But she wants something bigger. A meal, not a snack.

This place is perfect. Elderly owners away. No security. Down-and-out kind of street. I don't think anyone saw me sneak round the back, and, if they did, they probably don't care.

I empty the last of the first can over the kitchen floor. The petrol scampers to the edge of the room, finding gaps beneath the skirting board to settle in and wait. I take the second can upstairs; dribble a thin trail in my wake, to carry her. I anoint the walls around the landing, turning the wallpaper into touchpaper. The liquid pools on the lower lips of picture frames, beneath photos of smiling grandchildren. Strangers.

A splash across the clothes in the wardrobe drips from neatly pressed cuffs and matted fur collars. Satin skirts and silk ties turn shiny. Perfect white-cotton shirts take on an amber blush.

The concentrated fumes leave me giddy, my stomach churning. Or perhaps that's just anticipation. She's eager to begin, and I'm just as eager to please her. I want to watch her passion, her heat. Her satisfaction.

She's never truly satisfied, of course. I know that by now and it's what I love most about her. Her endless appetite, endless lust for destruction, endless capacity for creation.

When it started, all those years ago, one struck match could keep her sated for days. Then it was a box of matches, a garden bonfire. Growing attraction and con-nection, until that day, when we took our relationship to the next level.

On a piece of waste ground – a forsaken blind spot, surrounded by empty, graffiti-tagged warehouses – that I passed daily on my walk to and from school, someone had discarded a sofa. Stained, floral-patterned, a three-seater with sagging cushions and torn fabric.

She whispered of its potential: a glorious send off for the sorry-looking, unwanted piece of furniture. A pyre.

I stopped. Approached. Checked for witnesses even though I knew I was alone. I felt self-conscious, exposed, excited and scared at the same time. This wasn't like anything we'd tried before.

For kindling, I kicked a few paper cups, shreds of newspaper, fragments of splintered pallet wood, into a pile around the base of one arm. I withdrew my lighter from my pocket and rolled my thumb across the striker. A spark, and she emerged. I offered the flame to the frayed fringe around the sofa's base. Though it was dry as a bone, it took a while to catch – flame retardant, impregnated into the fabric. But she is relentless, determined, and eventually she latched on and began to spread. The fibres charred, curling and glowing red at the tips like fibre optics. Black smoke snaked up from the foam, which melted into a thick tar before igniting in earnest. The heat bathed my face. Noxious fumes and flakes of carbonised fabric, newspaper ash and sparks filled the air. I could taste it in the back of my mouth. My eyes stung, watered. But I couldn't take a single step back. I wanted the almost agony of being close to her, the sweat on my neck, the hot dry air filling my lungs, as she unleashed her full glorious self, just for me.

The wooden frame remained the longest, white-hot glowing bones inside an inferno that maintained the ghost-shape of the sofa long after the soft substance of it was gone. When that skeleton finally collapsed, the flames gave one last spark-filled leap skyward before settling down to consume the leftovers. Calm, languid. Sated.

For now.

I finished my journey home in a physical and emotional daze, awed by what I had just experienced. I finally understood what she really wanted; matches, candles, bonfires, barbecues, all things made to be burned, would never be enough. She only derives true pleasure from consuming that which was not destined for incineration. From that day we moved on and never looked back. Fences, cars, caravans, a children's climbing frame, we worked our way up to houses.

Houses have identity. Houses have soul. Houses can die.

I carefully pour a thin trickle of petrol over the chintz duvet. A pattern of red roses. Roses for my love. The fluid patters onto the fabric, pooling briefly where it takes a moment to soak in. Drips from the can splash into the tiny puddles, sending drops spinning across the surface like energetic ball bearings. Mesmerising.

Sirens.

I'm suddenly not sure how long they've been audible. How long have I stood here? But they're loud. Close. I cross to the window, peek out. No sign of vehicles on the street yet. I might have time to get out.

Don't leave, I need you.

Her whisper sends a shudder through me. The lighter in my pocket presses warm against my thigh.

I want this. I need it. Let me play.

I must go, now, but I hesitate. I won't have time to trail the last quarter of a can across the garden and release her. Even if I did, I wouldn't be able to stay and watch, and then really, what would be the point? She derives as much pleasure from my appreciation of her power, her beauty, as she does from the transformation of her fuel. My pleasure becomes hers and hers mine.

In the street the sirens approach. I've lingered too long, undone by indecision.

They'll take me away, she whispers.

No.

Yes. You know they will. They won't let you near so much as a single match for years.

"No." The word escapes my lips, into the room.

I'll find someone else.

"No. They won't catch me." I head for the door.

They will. It's too late.

I pause, hand on the door frame, legs shaking. I want her to be wrong but she's never wrong.

Unless…

Glancing at the petrol-soaked bed I feel her urge, her call, her desire.

"I can't. I'm afraid."

Yes, you can. Stay with me. Be with me. I'll help you.

Outside, a scrape of quick braking tyres on the road. A clang of doors opened and slammed shut. Voices shouting, but I don't register the words. I only hear her.

Quickly, she calls.

The sweet petrol fumes fill my mouth as I suck in rapid breaths. I can taste the unpleasant taint too, the truth beneath the lie. My skin itches. I climb onto the bed, kneel, hold the petrol can in trembling hands.

Don't be frightened. It was always meant to end this way. The pain will pass, I promise.

Lifting the can above my head I tilt it, slowly. Eyes closed. Mouth sealed tight shut. The liquid cascades through my hair, soaking into my collar. A trickle slides between my shoulder blades, like a lover's fingertips. It feels hot and cold at the same time. When the can is empty, I wipe my face with my sleeve and open my eyes. They burn, my lashes damp with petrol and tears.

It is an heretic that makes the fire,
Not she which burns in't.

~ SHAKESPEARE, THE WINTER'S TALE

Burning Desire

By Amanda Staples

'Tis almost a fortnight since I was sentenced to be hanged by the neck. I should be awaiting the gallows but instead I watch from my cell as they lay the pyre. The pyre they will now use to burn me at the stake. I've heard them chopping. I've seen them stack freshly cut wood and kindle gathered by children. They are purposely constructing it in sight of me.

I wonder if she will save me. I wonder if they have caught her too. I know she blames herself. She'd take my place if she could.

I am to be burned for sorcery. 'Twill be a highlight, a novelty, because it is uncommon for witches to be burned at the stake. It never happened in Salem. They were, all of them, hanged. All of them innocent like me. I am no witch. But she is.

Should I have done what I heard tell they did at the witch trials and plead guilty, repent my sins, name other witches? But I cannot repent something I see not as a sin.

And whom would I name? Not her. Never.

The last witch they hanged here in the marketplace came back to life. Sorcery, they said, of course. A bungled hanging, more like, by a hangman in his cups, a tavern landlord by day drinking the profits. I've seen a hanged man have his head jerked clean off his body. That is a sight you do not forget. So, now, I am to be burned, lest I resurrect myself. And the flames will cleanse my sin-tainted soul.

I cannot stop watching them build the pyre. My gaze will not be took from it. Like that decapitated hanged man, whose severed head I did not wish to look upon, yet could not but help myself. How macabre human nature is. I pray to the Goddess that they stack the wood evenly. I have been present at many a pyre but only one burning. I did not wish to attend but it was expected. Scaremongering and scapegoating had already begun so I had needs to be mindful. I stood apart from the baying crowd, close enough to be noticed, far enough away to slip into the woods. The pyre had been clumsily laid and as the fire took hold, it all but collapsed to one side. They say 'twas the devil trying to save her. She wore a woollen tunic. I know wool does not burn well. She died in agonies. The screams echoed in my head for days. Flames engulfed her unevenly. I turned away. I turned my back on her.

I will be burned in muslin.

The stench remains in my nostrils these three years hence. At first it is like pig roasting on a spit, then like charcoal and then a sickly-sweet smell. I burned sage and placed lavender about. There is no getting rid of the smell. Whenever we hear of a burning, we go at dusk. We check the set of the pyre; even it out, move kindle to the centre the better to burn. Once the feet are burned, death is quicker. More flames, more fire, with any luck you faint, then death. It is the least we can do. There are fewer burnings now; we are needed less. Hangings are cleaner, quicker, usually.

For the past month they have burned diseased animals and crops. Bad water it was. People died. I would not know how to hex, but that is what they claim and the blame lies at my door for all of it. For many things I could not and would not do. There is little point in protesting because what I am truly guilty of in their eyes cannot be spake of. The forbidden love. Unnatural, I am. To save the Elders of the church shame, I am instead branded a sorceress. I am accused of maleficium. I am sentenced to be destroyed by fire; cleansed by fire.

Am I to be took by the devil after all? Can a burned person still suffer in the flames of hell? My thoughts keep me awake until morn. Did she predict this with her oracle reading? Her divination? Did the hanged man appear in her Tarot? Though she has told me this does not mean death. If she is uncaptured she will save me. She will. I have to believe that. She is stealthy like a cloud passing over the moon.

In the mist of the early morning, they come for me. I know the wood on the pyre will be damp; 'twill not burn easily. Their grip is tight but I am shaking too much to struggle: from cold in my thin muslin, from fear.

They bind me; ropes criss-cross my torso, lashing me to the stake. I feel they would prefer to crucify me as they did their Christ, these Christians; all of them hypocrites and turncoats. Happy to avail themselves of my remedies when their loved ones took to bed with illness, happy to have me smooth the passage unto death with sedating herbs, happy to take my poultices and salves for fevered brows and souls. Now, they yank my hands behind my back and tie me roughly, without compassion. I retch. Bile rises. As they pull on the ropes they curse their lack of grip and I realise the fibres are not wet from dew. I can smell the animal fat. She has been. I know she will have checked the stacking of the wood and loaded kindle in the centre. Once it ignites, the flames will take hold. That's how our passion was for one another; a quick ignition followed by burning desire. Unstoppable. It made us less careful than we should have been.

The crowd is blurred through my tears; a muddle of jostling buckskin tunics and britches. I think I recognise voices as they jeer and spit and taunt but my heart is beating so fast a sloshing noise in my ears makes it diffi-cult to hear. I know there will be people present I called neighbour, friend. Family whose harvest I helped gather in, friends who cried on my shoulder, people I shared of my bread with and drew water for during the dark days.

I stand alone, but for her, if she be alive.

The fire is lit. I can smell it. Some kindle shifts, wood cracks and splits, heat rises. The soles of my feet prickle with the warmth. I think how we warmed our feet as we lay naked on the hearth in front of the fire. My toes curl reflexively against the increasing heat as though my feet are trying to retract into my ankles. Panic now. All thoughts gone. I shake like a tree in a storm and I am light-headed. With luck I will faint soon.

Fierce heat now. I think I may vomit. As smoke rises my vision clears then blurs again. I see her silhouette in a tricorn hat. I may be hallucinating. No. I watch as the figure shucks a cloak and lifts a bow and arrow. I know her from her stance. I know in my heart she is come. She pulls back her arm as I begin to scream. She is the best hunter I know. Her aim is as true as our love. She will pierce my heart for the second time.

Patience

BY BARRY HOLLOW

It stretches far, my human fuse,
which wears from traffic, much abused,
as tensile force with fury's zeal
is loaded fast and fierce to test,
with naught to say of when it passed.

Then, synapses stutter, sparks ignite,
blazes burn with blue arc flight!
And talk of ticking warning tocked,
the cool aplomb of patience snapped,
as light acquaints with heat, unlocked!
This incandescent essence flares,
with cataclysmic instant fire,
which catches those here on this site,
most unawares.

Now effect from cause has shown,
the charred confetti flutters round,
and remnants of my point are blown,
this scene of shock, needs kiss of life
for ruminations,
to lift the chars and indignation,
from cratered bowl of mindless doom.

Then spurs of sun, a burnished bronze,
give glimpse to push back clouds so dark,
and freeing wild spring hares to run
as apertures of ample sight,
are cleared of mist and scarlet hue.

The man who has been

beaten by a fire-brand dreads the

light of even a firefly.

~ SINHALESE PROVERB

Brand

By Alex Nicholas

In Eastwatch Cathedral the fire always burns atop the altar. It hasn't been allowed to die in over a hundred years, since an archbishop waved his crozier and pronounced consecration. Demek watches the flames dance in the golden vessel. They seem to yearn for the vast spaces under the vaulted roof; ever unsatisfied, their bound light flickers over gleaming surfaces.

Demek aches from kneeling on cold, polished stone. A thousand candles flicker in clusters at the ends of the pews. Behind the gilded altar, the great eastern window is empty and black. By day the cathedral floods with sunlight, but night has long since fallen. Demek's fellow initiates are scattered through the nave. Each is alone. It's their vigil night, and in the morning on midsummer's day they'll become full members of the Church. They'll be branded with the sign of the Rising Sun at dawn.

The brazier sits squat and dark on the dais, its black iron bars twisted into the wings and haloes of blazing angels. Demek's eyes linger on the branding iron. He shivers. Celestial beings rejoice in that searing kiss, but human flesh recoils.

Footsteps shatter the heavy silence. Demek lowers his head as the sound draws near. *Please, deacon, pass me by. I'm nothing but obedient.* He only looks up when he feels a hand on his shoulder. It's no deacon standing there; this man is cloaked and hooded in dark cloth.

"Herdsmen brand their cattle, you know," the man whispers. "On the Veldia Isles they brand slaves."

Demek takes a sharp breath. He knows that voice. Demek's brother Samshen fled his own vigil night two years before, signed on a merchant ship the next day in Eastwatch docks. Broke their mother's heart, as she reminds Demek every chance she gets. She says it to strengthen his resolve, but it makes him shrivel. His parents bear the Rising Sun with pride. Demek's barely seen his brother since he left home, a snatched visit here or there, away from disapproving eyes.

They'd been inseparable once. Working side by side in their father's cordwainer shop, cutting and stitching the leather. Demek used to watch Samshen charm the nobles' daughters who came in and wonder where the hells he got the confidence. Later they'd sit before the hearth, Demek open mouthed as Samshen told him tales of the butchers' girls, and where they'd let you put your hands if you were nice to them. *Was any of it true?*

Samshen walks on, quick and furtive. Demek stares after him, slack-jawed, stunned by his sudden presence. Samshen glances back, beckons with a crook of his fingers.

It's not hard to guess what he wants to say, and there's a part of Demek that doesn't want to hear it. *As if this isn't hard enough already.* Still, he follows.

They pass through a door in a wooden screen behind the choir stalls. It's carved with scenes from the lives of the saints, and all Demek can see are the vivid depictions of flames, central in every panel.

Past the screen, Samshen hurries through the empty transept. At the northern point of the cathedral is the chapel of Saint Mechel, last martyr of Sacreth. A portrait of the Saint hangs above the altar, his features hard and uncompromising, lit from below by another altar fire.

"Listen," Samshen says, "I've been where you are. You stare at the brazier and wonder how much it will hurt. They want you to feel that pain because they have. You're not supposed to cry out, but will you? You think you've no choice, but you have, Demek. You have."

Samshen pushes back his hood. *He looks so tired.* His eyes are intense, blazing sincerity, but the lines beneath them are etched deep.

"I'm moving to Windhollow. Things are different there. The Church is almost powerless in the Queen's city, you can choose a new god. Men and women drink side by side in the taverns. There's freedom, and it's bloody wonderful."

He takes a deep breath. "Come with me, Demek. We can start together, our own business, not like we don't know what we're doing. We can be happy there. They want to own every bit of you, they burn their mark into your skin and you'll never be rid of them. We all want to belong, but it's too much."

The sound of footsteps comes from deeper in the cathedral, muffled but growing louder. Samshen's head jerks round. There's fear in his eyes. *If they find him here, what will they do?*

Samshen grips Demek's shoulder. "Come and find me at the Three Ships," he says. "I miss you. Don't let this be the end for us."

"I miss you too," Demek says, or tries to say. This night, of all nights, he can't find his voice. He raises a hand in silent farewell, staring after Samshen as he slips away through the chapel door. Alone, again.

Saint Mechel watches him, and Demek sees judgement in that painted gaze. Was Mechel scared before he took the brand? That small suffering was nothing compared to what awaited him, but that doesn't make it meaningless. After the saint was hanged, his followers stole his body in the night. They made a pyre and sent his soul to the Bright Halls. His ashes sit in a silver jar.

Demek stares at the altar and sees a reflection of god burning upon it. The Dawnfather blazes brighter than any fire, radiant and harsh in equal measure. His character is written in the marrow of his Church. They'll mark Demek's flesh and his soul too, and abruptly he knows. *It isn't what I want.*

The chapel spins around him. He clutches at a chair, vomit rising in his throat. If he walks out now it's his whole life, it's family meals with his parents and sisters, it's sweating in the shop to finish a design and the spreading tingle of pride when his father praises the work. It's the feeling he gets when Elina the carpenter's daughter looks at him that certain way. It's a life he wants, at a price that seems staggeringly high.

Demek bites his lip as footsteps ring behind him. A hand grips his shoulder, and his whole body clenches as he turns. It's one of the deacons, robed in light grey. He's frowning. Demek dredges his memory for a name and can't find one.

"Initiates are to remain within the nave," the deacon says.

"Sorry. I didn't think anyone would mind. I just… "

Demek's voice trails into silence in the face of the deacon's stern expression. *There's nothing I can say he'll understand.*

"I'm to fetch you for confession. We mustn't keep the Lightbringer waiting."

He leads Demek back to the nave. At the far end, the great cathedral doors are open, flanked by blazing torches. There's a world beyond them that Demek doesn't understand. He glances at the altar fire. Too close and it will burn you, too far and you're out in the cold, alone.

The confessional box is halfway down the nave, tucked behind a pillar, sunken in a deep pool of shadow. Its wood is plain and unadorned, simple against a backdrop of shining marble and gold.

The deacon shoves Demek over the threshold, and the heavy bone-white curtain falls into place behind him. A near-total darkness envelops him. Stifling air constricts his throat. His reaching fingers scrabble against lacquered wood, and his breath comes hard.

"It may not be the most welcoming place, Demek, but

you're quite safe. Please, be seated."

It's Lightbringer Marlow, Demek's parish priest. Demek's seen him glowering from the pulpit, eyes stabbing accusation as he thundered threats of damnation in frozen hells. His voice then hard as wrought-iron nails, but now it's mellow and reassuring.

"Your confession doesn't really interest me, I'm afraid. I'd like you to tell me what your brother said to you."

Demek's fingers dig into his palms. As his eyes grow accustomed to the gloom of the confessional, he sees the stark lines of the metal grill between him and the priest.

"How do you know he was here?"

Marlow chuckles. "He's not exactly subtle, is he? It doesn't matter anyway, I expect I can guess the line. The Church wants to own your life, and we brand you like cattle to keep you corralled. He said that if you go through the Dawning, you'll never be free, is that it?"

Demek nods dumbly, but of course the priest can't see the gesture. He draws a deep breath, searching for a scrap of his brother's courage. *If I say nothing now then I never will.*

"He's right though, isn't he?" His voice is small, but it's his.

Marlow sighs. "He came to me with those concerns two years and more ago, and the Dawnfather knows I've heard it before. I'm afraid I offered him platitudes that in the end were apparently of no comfort. To you I'll give the truth as I see it, and if you still can't face it you're free to go, of course. You're free to do a lot of things, but it doesn't mean they're good for you."

The confessional smells of polish and the heady sweetness of scented candles. They burn on Marlow's side, beyond the grill and a barrier of heavy cloth. *He probably sits on a velvet cushion too.*

"Samshen turned his back on the church," Marlow says, "but I doubt he found the freedom he dreamed of. It doesn't exist, you know, not for any of us and certainly not for him. From the moment you're born your parents make all your decisions, they own pieces of you. Yet your very presence curtails their freedoms, creating endless demands on their time. Chains of obligation run both ways.

"By casting himself adrift, your brother only re-forged the links. The captain of his ship, his crewmates, his landlord, he owed them all. They all had their hooks in him. People he's never met had a say over his life, ruling his fate with the stroke of a pen. All he achieved was to cut himself off from the people who love him.

"Now he's lost his berth, did he tell you that? They kicked him out, and he's desperate. Don't let him drag you down as well."

Wood creaks as the priest shifts his weight. Demek can't believe he's here, facing the coming dawn. He thinks of the branding iron and wishes the years would roll back.

"I don't think I can do it," he says softly. He doesn't know if he means he can't leave, or he can't stay. Both seem impossible.

"You're not a child anymore," Marlow says. "Don't forget, I've been where you are. I know how it feels. I thought I'd faint when they brought me to the brazier, but I didn't. I didn't make a sound and neither will you. I'll be honest with you here. I don't want to stay a parish priest forever. The Church is powerful and wealthy. You give us your flesh today, but don't say we offer nothing in return.

"What Samshen did hurt me. There are hooks in me too, you see Demek. I wear more brands than you're ever likely to. It's the same all the way up the chain. Even the Dawnson has to answer, and nobody is free. The only decision is which set of irons to wear and I promise you'll be better off with the church. We run Eastwatch. The fire burns, but you'll heal. Better that than the darkness."

A long silence settles on the confessional. At some point, Demek surfaces from fevered reverie to realise the priest is gone. In the dark, behind the curtain, it feels like the last safe space, like he can stop time and never have to say, one way or another. Was Samshen brave, or stupid?

I wish I knew.

But the sun always rises, and inertia is as much a decision as a headlong rush into the night. He forces himself to his feet.

Back in the nave, the vastness dizzies him. All that weight of air presses down and he can't breathe. He staggers along, touching the heads of pews as he passes. His vision blurs as tears spring to his eyes.

The cathedral doors frame the night; there's nothing between Demek and the unbound world. He grips the wooden frame and teeters there, at the threshold between his life and the unknown. The square outside is blanketed in darkness, but on the far side windows glow bright with hearth-light. The Bishop of Eastwatch's residence, a beacon of radiance.

There are so many rules in the Church that make so little sense. People to obey, and be obeyed by; Demek wants neither. *But can I give up everything I know? A whole existence, against what? A brother and an ideal. Freedom's not real anyway, it's a child's story. Say it enough times, I might start to believe it.*

In the end, he cannot take that final step. He'll never know what life he could have had. Is it cowardice, or something else? He looks up at the stars, and lets the tears roll down his cheeks.

At dawn, when the sun rises over the sea and the east window glows orange behind the altar, Demek kneels. He's one in a long line of initiates. The Bishop of Eastwatch stands beside the brazier, holding the branding iron in a white-gloved hand. He weaves a pattern in the air as he intones a prayer in High Dwellan. Demek doesn't understand the language, but it doesn't matter. He can't take his eyes off that length of blackened metal. It ends in a semi-circle, the sun on the horizon. It ends in a new beginning.

Demek's parents are watching, somewhere in the endless crowd behind him, but he can't think about that. He can't think about Samshen, or the ache he knows will never fully go away. He'd pray for his brother, but he doesn't know who to pray to.

His fellows go, one by one, to the altar. He knows their faces, some of them are his friends but today he can't seem to recognise any of them, all he sees are arms bared and metal glowing red. Some of them flinch, some roar their pain. One faints. He's branded anyway, lying on the stone floor, a hiss and a wisp of smoke rising from his arm. His back arches. The deacons drag him away.

When it's his turn, Demek's feet take him. He kneels with the Bishop looming over him and wonders how he got there. The Bishop's gut strains at his dazzling robe. The smell of smoke and scorched meat threatens to overwhelm.

"In the name of the Dawnfather and his son Emyr, I welcome Demek into our church."

The branding iron rests in the brazier, surrounded by smouldering coals. Heat presses against Demek's cheek.

"May you serve faithfully and well all your life, until he welcomes you into his Bright Halls. You kneel a child, you rise as one of us. A brother."

The Bishop lifts the iron. It smokes. Demek closes his eyes. He sways, breathing shallow and fast. Sweat slides down his back.

Pain hits Demek like nothing he's felt before, a pure white moment of agony. Lights explode behind his eyes. He doesn't flinch, he doesn't make a sound, just as he's been told.

Inside, he's screaming.

The Devil's Handmaidens

By Maria Herring

I

"The fearefull aboundinge at this time in this countrie, of these detestable slaves of the Devill, the Witches or enchaunters,…merits most severly to be punished."

Daemonologie, King James I, 1597

You didn't want to come, but your father insisted. No one argues with your father, especially not you.

There's a festival air, which makes you blink. One of the local farmers has spit a pig, roasts it over a small bonfire. The air is greasy with the stench of burning fat. Groups of villagers stand about, talking and laughing, delighted to have a legitimate reason not to work. Ecstatic to be able to join in with the gossip without being the cause of it. A pack of barefoot children brandishing sticks chases a stray dog around the village, adding to the clamour. You want to cover your ears every time one clubs the beast and makes it squeal, but you don't want to draw your father's attention. You don't want to draw anyone's attention. Not today of all days. Not when the Devil's handmaidens are taking up so prominent a place in the village square.

Yesterday was June 19th, the year of our Lord 1646. You know that because your father took you to the local assizes court and the judge proclaimed it before the trial started. Usually you don't pay too much attention to the individual days, the seasons suffice. You know it's autumn when your father's neighbours are getting the harvest in. You know it's winter because you celebrate the birth of Jesus Christ. You know it's spring when your father's farmhands are busy with the lambing. You know it's summer when the village celebrates the solstice. Usually days are irrelevant. Except this one.

"Got to have the trial before the Solstice," your father said. "Only the Devil knows what tricks his handmaidens would play on us if we left them to it."

He took you to watch. Said it was important to see how men of God dealt with the wicked. None of it made sense to you yesterday, and it still doesn't today. Why would the Devil's handmaidens cause more trouble on the longest day of the year? They prefer darkness to light, that's what everyone says. But since that night when your father discovered the first handmaiden in your village, you stopped trying to make sense of anything.

II

"A great nomber of them that ever have bene convict or confessors of Witchcraft are...altogether given over to the pleasures of the flesh."

Daemonologie, King James I, 1597

Tilly arrived at the farmhouse a year after your mother died from a fever. At 13, she was only two years older than you, but she took care of you as fondly as mother ever did. And you were grateful to have help with the household chores. Your father belted you bitterly after a night in his cups, said the cost of hiring and boarding a housemaid was your fault. Said you never pulled your weight around the place, even though your calluses said otherwise. Your beatings were less frequent with Tilly there, because all the work got done.

Fear still shadowed you, though. Not for your own safety; for hers. At dinner times, father would glare at Tilly with the same expression of lust and disgust that once fell on you. That once petrified you. Would he beat her now instead of you? Perhaps as well as. That would be your fault. She was only here because of you.

And so, one night, you heard your father clatter downstairs to Tilly's cot by the hearth. You covered your ears under your blanket to shut out the screams you knew would follow –

– but it was your father who screamed instead. A roar

of rage so fearful it made your belly hurt. You dreaded what would happen to Tilly the following morning at breakfast, but father was no more gruff than usual. Still, you noticed the way he stared at her when she turned away to get more porridge from the pot over the fireplace. Saw the scheming in his eyes. So it wasn't a surprise when he started keeping vigil on the upstairs landing. Sitting in darkness at the top of the stairs, watching Tilly leave in the middle of the night, leafing through his battered copy of *Demonologie* by candlelight, watching her come back in an hour before breakfast. He did nothing, said nothing, for a whole week.

And then one night, he followed her out. Part of you was relieved, because at least you wouldn't hear anything. But when the door creaked open again only a few minutes later, your belly twisted again.

Except, he didn't have Tilly with him; he had two of his farm-hands. You didn't know their names, because father would never let you speak to them. But, sitting on the top of the stairs in the dark now, like your father had done all week, you recognised them alright. Both tall, both solid as oxen. One had dirty blond hair and icy blue eyes, and you called him Saxon. You could just imagine his ancestors storming the shores and harrying the Britons. The other had red hair and freckles. Everyone in the village called him Irish, even though he wasn't. You knew the three of them were waiting for Tilly to come home, and your belly told you that you didn't want to be sitting on top of these stairs when she did; but you couldn't move your legs. You kept telling yourself there was hours to go until she came back anyway. Only, the door opened and in she walked.

There was a moment of shock when she saw the three figures lit up by the fire. When her eyes landed on Irish they showed confusion.

Then your father spoke. "Where do you go at night?"

She shook her head, but you didn't think it was an answer. You thought she was trying to shake away her confusion.

"Where do you go at night?" your father repeated. His voice was calm and quiet. That meant his fury was deep and cold.

Tilly's gaze whipped across to Irish for just a second, then dropped to the floor.

"Lads," your father said, gesturing towards Tilly with his head.

She screamed then, before either had even touched her, a scream of pure terror because she knew her life was firmly in the hands of men.

Once Irish and Saxon had firm grasp of her arms, they dragged her across the flagstone floor, swept clean by Tilly, and thrust her upper body down onto the large oaken table. You remember your mother's pride of that table, the way she told you how her father had carved it as a wedding present for her. Tilly's face landed on it with a crunch, and as you winced at the sound, you saw Irish wince too. You saw your father smirk.

"Where do you go at night?" he said.

"Nowhere, I promise!" Tilly wailed.

"Last month," he said, "you healed the child with

herbs." He was talking about you. "How did you do that?"

"I… I, what?" You couldn't see Tilly's face anymore. She was facing the hearth and Saxon's calloused hand kept it fixed in place. You heard the confusion in her voice though. She sounded as confused as you felt. What did your fever have to do with anything?

"You healed the child with herbs last month," your father said. The strain of keeping his voice calm was starting to show. His knuckles were white where they clutched *Demonologie* to his heart. "How did you do it? Was it witchcraft?"

"No!" Tilly shrilled.

"Where do you go at night? Do you cavort with the devil?"

"No! I swear it!" She started to cry. "I don't understand!"

"Are you a witch?"

"No!"

"Confess, girl, and I'll go easy on you." Your father had used those words before, and you've never believed him. Tilly probably didn't either.

"I'm not a witch, I swear it!" she shrieked.

Your father nodded at the two lads, and Irish bent to a sack on the floor, while Saxon increased the pressure on poor Tilly's head. You felt like you should run down the stairs. Not to do or say anything especially, but just because your presence might make the men think twice about what they were doing if a child were present. You thought about it. But you did nothing.

Then Irish attached something chunky and metal to the edge of your mother's oaken table, and in the firelight you saw splinters pop out where the metal bit in. You frowned. You didn't know what it was.

Then he took Tilly's hand in both of his and started dragging it towards the thing on the table. She must have guessed what it was, because her screaming started afresh.

"No, no, no! Please! I didn't do anything! Tell them!"

You wondered briefly who she was talking to, but then you saw Irish place Tilly's fingers in between two narrow, metal plates. She writhed and screeched, and even though you knew she had fair strength in her, she was no match for Irish and Saxon.

Once her fingers were between the plates, Irish clamped down on her wrist, then started twisting a screw down on the top plate, pushing it towards the bottom plate. With Tilly's fingers in the middle. Your belly lurched when you realised what the metal thing was. How did your father get his hands on a pilliwinks?

You closed your eyes, because you couldn't bear to see Tilly's fingers shatter.

"Are you a witch?" You father kept asking this, over and over, but Tilly didn't answer. How could they expect her to answer when she was in so much pain?

Finally, Irish released her hand and you were relieved. It was over. But when Tilly denied she was a witch again, your father made Irish screw Tilly's other hand. And still she denied. You wondered how much pain a person could endure. Could you have endured this? Would you have already confessed just to make the pain stop? How could Tilly bear it?

The grey light of dawn crept along the landing to where

you sat. Your father and his farm-hands tortured Tilly throughout the night, but still she didn't confess.

"I know you're a handmaiden of the devil, whore!" your father finally screamed, brandishing his book in her face. "If you won't confess with words, I'll find evidence with marks! Strip her!"

You were astonished that Tilly still had fight left in her, as Saxon and Irish began tearing at her clothes. She couldn't use her hands, because they were shattered beyond use, but she used her elbows, until your father gave her such a blow to the head that she swooned. Irish caught her, snapping the bones of her corset as he did so, and revealing a round, blood red mark above her left breast. He looked at it guiltily, then peered into Tilly's face.

"Please confess, Tilly," Irish said. He sounded scared to you. "Then we'll stop. But you have to confess. Please."

She looked back at him, shaking her head and sobbing. But this time it wasn't the weeping of a girl in physical pain. This was heartbreak pain. You'd seen that look in mother's face plenty of times, before and after a beating from your father.

"Please, Tilly," Irish whispered.

She never stopped shaking her head, but her next words made tears start from your eyes.

"I made a covenant with the Devil," she said, voice thick with tears and torment. "I would go out in the middle of the night and dance naked on the heath, and let the devil have his way with me." Your father let out a triumphant roar and smashed his fist down on your mother's oaken table.

"But it wasn't just me," Tilly said with a sigh. "I was part of a coven."

The three men looked at each other, mouths agape. You were wide awake now, even though dawn was breaking and you hadn't slept all night.

Then Tilly reeled off a list of names of people you'd never heard before. They were all women's names. Except for the last one. "James Shepherd," she said.

Irish's arms fell limply to his sides. "Tilly," he whispered, face deathly white in the firelight. "What've you done?"

"You're the Devil himself, James Shepherd," she said, fat tears still rolling down her cheeks. "Look what you did to me. Look what you let *them* do to me. You did nothing to help me. How could I possibly leave you unnamed?"

III

"…(the Devill) gives them his marke upon some secreit place of their bodie, which remaines soare unhealed…"

Daemonologie, King James I, 1597

You look at Tilly now. She's first to be brought out amongst the spectators enjoying their festival. They boo and hiss at her as she's dragged. Her face is mostly white, which makes the violet marks of violence from that night a fortnight ago stand out all the more starkly. She doesn't struggle today. Doesn't even flinch when half-eaten food smacks her in the face, leaving trails of grease down her cheeks. The spectators laugh and cheer. You want to cry, but you keep your tears in check. Your father isn't looking at you, but you know he's watching you.

Men shout "Satan's whore!" and women shout "burn her!" and you keep silent. Not only is your father watching, the whole village is. Desperately keeping their eyes open for another witch in their midst. After the trials at the assizes yesterday, no one's safe. Those king's men who aren't busy with the prisoners are milling about the cheering crowds, looking out for signs of witchcraft.

Tilly's led to the stake, her lifeless arms tied at the back. But there's more than one stake. You know how to count, because your mother taught you your letters and numbers, but you don't want to count them. You don't want to count how many will die because of yesterday.

IV

(The Devill) oblishes him selfe to appeare at their calling upon him…either in the likeness of a dog, a Catte, an Ape, or such-like other beast."

Daemonologie, King James I, 1597

The assizes court was packed to the rafters. You'd never been here before. It was a day-and-a-half's ride away to the town, so of course you'd never seen it before. You'd never even been to town before. When you finally arrived, your father rode directly to the castle, looking perfectly at ease on top of his horse amongst the bustle, looking down at the peasants who had to get to the castle on foot.

The castle terrified you. Reaching it meant crossing a stone walkway over a vast moat, towards a turreted tower. In the light of the red dawn, you imagined you were walking across the tongue of a slavering mouth. When you passed under the barbican, the raised portcullis glinted like teeth.

Once inside the courtyard, all was lost to the clamour and confusion of too much humanity, the stench of horse shit, and a fog of flies. You saw your father leap off his horse and hand the reins to a stable lad, so you hurried to do the same, always keeping your eyes on him. You didn't want to get lost in here. Your father's fine woollen cloak, dyed black as raven feathers, became your entire world. You couldn't grab hold of it, it was too expensive for that, so you blocked out everything else and kept your eyes fixed on it. When your father finally turned around to speak to you, you'd made it through the labyrinth of the castle into the court room where the assizes took place.

"Now you'll see how God's men mete out justice to the wicked," he said with a sneer. And also a threat.

Everywhere smelt of old wood, beeswax and stale sweat. Excited chattering from the benches behind you bounced off the wooden panelling lining the vast chamber, but the two sombre men seated at the judge's bench had their heads close together, no doubt sharing their arcane secrets of law. One of them caught you staring and his face remained as wooden as the walls behind him. You would have preferred a scowl to that lack of emotion.

His colleague called the court to order, and the bailiff brought in the accused. Many of them were old women you didn't recognise. As the bailiff read out their names and where they came from, you realised that they weren't just people from your village, but from all over the county. You were about to witness a mass witch trial.

When Tilly stumbled up onto the witness bench your belly took a tumble. Her eyes seemed to have grown too large for her face, and she cradled her broken hands in front of her chest. The only man in the stand was Irish, James Shepherd, and he appeared just as frightened and filthy as all the women. You noticed the two judges raised their eyebrows at each other when James took his place next to Tilly.

The last person to enter was Old Widow Clarke. Old Widow Clarke? You looked up at your father to ask why she was there too, but he was mumbling curses at all the accused, just as all the other spectators were. You turned back to her. She blinked around the court in obvious con-fusion, fingers twisting together in anguish, mumbling to herself and sobbing into her hands frequently. Pity poked at your heart. You mother had always liked the old widow. She'd always taken over a pot of stew once a week to make sure she had something hot to eat.

"But she's mean," you remembered telling your mother once. "She shouts at everyone in the village."

"She's a cantankerous old biddy," your mother had

said. "But that's just because she's frightened and alone and old. You wouldn't be here if it weren't for Old Widow Clarke, and nor would most of the rest of the village. We can't forget our old folk just because they've forgotten themselves."

You couldn't decide if your mother was brave or silly, because you'd thought Old Widow Clarke was the scariest person in the world.

Exclamations of surprise susurrated around the court, pulling you out of your reverie. A little girl now stood centre stage. You recognised her. She was called Alice, and her father was Saxon. She was younger than you by two years. Her hair was hidden under a straw bonnet, tied under her chin with a yellow ribbon. Her dress was white cotton. You'd never seen her look so clean.

"Old Mother Widow is a witch," Alice said. The spectators gasped their shock and delight. "I did see her conjure up a brown dog, she did call him Ball. And I did hear her ask him to help her with murders."

The crowd was silent now, riveted by little Alice's speech.

"And who did she murder?" asked one of the judges.

"Old Man Devis, who lives by the meadow," Alice said. "And Simple Tom, who got run over by a cart the next day. And she did curse my father. I did see her make a clay man, and she did use it to curse my father, and the next week, two of the sheep he looks after did die."

"Curse that whore of Satan," your father hissed, glaring at Old Widow Clarke. Then he launched himself off the bench, wielding *Demonologie* like a weapon. "They were my sheep you killed! My sheep!"

The spectators around you mumbled their approval at this unexpected witness, but the judges were less impressed.

"Order! I will have order!" said one, banging his hand on the bench. The crowd settled down quickly enough, but you couldn't keep your eyes off Old Widow Clarke.

She was cantankerous, yes, but she didn't look mean enough to kill sheep, let alone people. And she didn't seem to understand what people were saying about her either. She kept to turning to Tilly, asking her to explain, but Tilly just stared blankly at the floor. Eventually, she stopped listening altogether and just sobbed quietly into her hands.

You wanted to jump up and say something in her defence. How all the people in the village used to like her before she was Old Widow Clarke, when she was just Mrs Clarke, who knew all the herbs that could help treat simple illnesses. How she'd helped all the babies of the village be born. How your mother used to like her and look after her, before she'd died. But the judge had shouted at your father, and he was a man. What would he do to a child?

So you did nothing.

V

"…for as that sexe is frailer then men is, so is it easier to be entrapped in these grosse snares of the Devill, as was over well proved to be true, by the Serpents deceiving of Eva at the beginning."

Daemonologie, King James I, 1597

When Old Widow Clarke is brought out to her stake, the two king's men have to carry her because she's only got one leg. People standing nearest to her think this is hilarious and laughter patters across the village green.

Just like Tilly, Old Widow Clarke has lost all her fight. Her skin is sallow and bruised, and she's shivering like it's the bleak midwinter rather than midsummer's day.

Other women are brought out soon after, women you recognise from the trial but not all of them from your village. James Shepherd isn't there. He was acquitted because of lack of evidence against him. This pleased your father. Three other women from neighbouring villages were also acquitted for the same reason. This didn't please your father. Before he left the court that day he waved his copy of *Demonologie* up at the judges, but they didn't notice. Or they pretended not to. Your father's important in your village, but too small for the likes of town judges.

The last person they bring out is a little girl. Orphan Jennet, people call her. She's a beggar in your village. She's always been there. You don't know how old she is, because you never spoke to her. She always frightened you a little bit, because her face is strange. Her eyes are too big, and she's got a bulge coming out of her left temple. People said that her parents abandoned her because they were ashamed of her deformity. You don't know if this is true. You didn't see her at the trial, so you don't understand why she's here today.

"Because she's always surrounded by her familiars," says your father after you ask him. "Cats and dogs wherever she goes. Always summoning them. One look at her and you know she's the Devil's child."

You'd always thought those cats and dogs were just strays. The village had plenty to spare, what with all the farmlands hereabouts. You thought it was kind the way she'd beg for food in the village, and then share it with all the other creatures that were just as abandoned as she was. And how could she summon them anyway? She couldn't even speak properly.

She spoke to you once, little orphan Jennet. Some bigger boys had beaten you for fun, and ripped the new cloak that your mother had stitched for your birthday. You didn't want to go home because you knew she'd be upset with you. So you just sat in the curb, crying into your hands, wishing you were bigger so that you could fight back.

Then a hand tapped you on the shoulder. It was little Jennet. She had a bunch of wild flowers in her hand and was holding them out to you. She was trying to say something, but you couldn't make out the words. You could tell, though, that she wanted you to take the flowers. So you did. She beamed at you with such happiness it made you feel happy too.

Of course, when you got home, your mother was upset and your father whipped you soundly for ripping an expensive new cloak, but you never forgot little Jennet's kindness.

It doesn't make sense to you that someone who cares for miserable creatures the way she always does could be a witch.

You look at all the women now, tied to their stakes. You know you should be scared of them because they're witches. Judges said that they've done terrible evils because they're handmaidens of the Devil. But apart from Tilly and Jennet who are young, they all just look like poor, scared, old women to you. If they were so evil and powerful, why weren't they using their magic to get free of the stakes? At this moment, it seems to you that every old woman with a wrinkled face, a furrowed brow, hairy lip, a gobber tooth, a squint eye, a squeaking voice, or a scolding tongue, and a dog or cat by her side is not only suspected, but pronounced for a witch.

You see the executioner step up behind Tilly with his garrotte. He's a fat man, paid well to take the lives of others, then feasts on their deaths. She twitches a little, Tilly, when the rope's pulled tight, but that's all. All the fight went out of her that night in your house when you watched from the top of the stairs.

But the other women are in mortal fear of their fates now, when they see the executioner untwist his rope and step away from Tilly's stake. Their wailing starts up, but is drowned out by the cheers and applause of the spectators as the first witch in their midst is dispatched. You look around at them. You understand that they're pleased to be rid of evil, because you're scared of evil too. Except, for you it's always been a nameless, faceless thing that kept you well-behaved for your parents and made sure you went to church every Sunday. It never had the face of someone you knew. Not even your father. Because everyone in the village knew Tilly and Old Widow Clarke and little orphan Jennet. They never used to be evil before. People were never afraid of them before. Why now?

You can't take the sneers and jubilations any more. You look back at the women, feeling that it's your duty to be a witness for them. Let them know that there's at least one person who's not celebrating. Because what must it feel like, to look out at a sea of faces you've known all your life, and watch them cheer as the breath is slowly squeezed out of your body?

Your eyes catch those of little Jennet. She blinks at you, mouths something, words you probably wouldn't understand anyway even if you could hear her. But you see in her face that she's asking for help. It's written clearly in the dark circles that terror has drawn around her eyes, in the quiver in her mouth, and the twitching of her head.

You see yourself run up to the stake she's bound to. See yourself rip apart the knots in the rope at her wrists. See yourself fend off the angry villagers while she makes her escape across the village green, explaining to them that she's just a little girl, and nothing to be afraid of.

You see this clearly, and it pleases you. Pleases you that you've done something. So when little Jennet's tongue lolls out of her mouth followed by a hideous rasping of final breath, you blink rapidly. When her cheeks turn blue and her eyes bulge, your eyes fill with tears. But… but you helped her. Didn't you?

No. You did nothing.

VI

"They ought to be put to death according to the Law of God…by fire."

Daemonologie, King James I, 1597

When the flames climb, even the spectators stop cheering. The air is filled with the stench of burning human fat. The smoke burns your eyes, stings your throat. You feel its tendrils wrapping around the strands of your hair, penetrating the weave in your clothes. You feel the weight of it dragging you down. You know you'll never be rid of the reek of it. You look at your father, but he's wandered off to the pig roast, *Demonologie* still clutched in his right hand. The heat and stink of burning witches crisps your hair so you move away, follow your father. What else can you do?

Thirty-four Matches on the Rising Scale of Happiness

By Clare Dornan

One badly burnt finger!

Two candles lit for make-up dinner. Meal burnt.

Fight continues.

One red wax stained tablecloth. Wedding present from his parents.

First use and it's ruined.

Three failed attempts to light the barbecue. Damp coals. Told to buy new ones, but he always knows better.

Two birthday cake candles blown out by the wind. Toddler inconsolable.

Party is a bloody disaster.

Two tea-lights on the bath edge. Lights off, time to relax.

Knocked into the water on entry.

One gas hob ignition re-light. Old stove condemned, dinner is saved.

One first-strike lighting of the barbecue (in front of the in-laws).

Two home-carved flying witch pumpkin lanterns.

Three late night cigarettes (shared).

One firelight hand-shadow performance on the garden wall.

Five sparklers.

Three birthday candles and perfect toddler candle-blow-out. #he's3already!

Two bonfires on the beach, marshmallow kebabs, sticky fingers and sandy toes.

One camping stove, post-cold-swim. Hands around hot cups, three huddle close.

Three candles, romantic dinner for two (you know, you still look alright in low light).

One candle relit for breakfast in bed.

About the Authors

B. Anne Adriaens

B. Anne Adriaens currently lives in Somerset. Her work tends to reflect her interest in alienation and all things weird and dark, as well as her concerns about the environment. She's written several dystopian prose pieces and is finalising her first poetry collection. You can read her in *Helios Quarterly*, *Harpur Palate*, *Glasgow Review of Books*, *Whirlagust* (The Yaffle Prize 2019, for which she was awarded third prize), *Thimble Magazine*, *The Blue Nib*, *Poetry Ireland Review*, *The Honest Ulsterman*, *Bloody Amazing!* (an anthology breaking one of the oldest taboos surrounding women) and *Rat's Ass Review*.

Photographs of places which inspired her, and random quirkiness she felt compelled to capture, can be found on her Flickr page:

www.flickr.com/photos/b-anne-adriaens/

Dev Agarwal

Dev Agarwal writes dark fantasy, near future science fiction and horror. He has published fiction in print and on line in a variety of magazines.

Dev is editor of *Focus*, the British Science Fiction Association's magazine for genre writers. He also writes non fiction on line and for both *Focus* and *Vector* magazines (published by the BSFA).

Dev is currently at work drafting his first novel.

Clare Dornan

Clare Dornan's stories have been published online and in *North by Southwest* and *Tales from the Graveyard*. She's currently working on an anthology of shorts and flash fiction. For a day job she produces and directs science, wildlife and adventure programmes and many of her fictional characters are inspired by the people she meets when filming.

She can be found on Instagram: **@clared129**

Chrissey Harrison

Chrissey Harrison writes books about monsters, magic, action and adventure, and fragile human characters trying to muddle through as best they can.

Her debut novel, *Mime,* released in 2020, the first in her *Weird News* Series. Her short stories have appeared in several anthologies, most recently *Forgotten Sidekicks* from Grimbold Books.

When she's not writing books, she's often making them, both as a freelance graphic designer and a craft bookbinder.

Website:
chrisseyharrison.com

Twitter & Instagram:
@ChrisseyWrites

Chloe Headdon

Chloe grew up wanting to be either a writer or a knight, but since dressing up in armour and swinging a sword around isn't a viable life plan (apparently), she completed an English degree and a Masters in Medieval Studies before going on to work in marketing.

Chloe writes fantasy and speculative fiction, with stories published in *Holdfast Magazine* and North Bristol Writers' *Tales from the Graveyard*. She has also been a guest reader at BristolCon Fringe and Weston Writers' Nights. She is currently busy with her debut young adult fantasy novel, set in the same world as *Esau's Gift*.

In her spare time, Chloe pursues her sword-wielding dreams as a student of Historical European Martial Arts (HEMA) and as a medieval re-enactor, both of which come in handy when writing fight scenes.

Follow her on Twitter:
@ChloeHeaddon

Kevlin Henney

Kevlin Henney writes shorts and flashes and drabbles of fiction and books and articles on software development.

His fiction has appeared online and on tree (*Daily Science Fiction, Litro, New Scientist, Physics World, Reflex Fiction, LabLit, Flight Journal* and many more) and has been included in a number of anthologies (*Tales from the Graveyard, The Dark Half of the Year, North by Southwest, We Can Improve You, Haunted, Salt Anthology of New Writing, Ripening, Sleep Is a Beautiful Colour* and many more).

He lives in Bristol and online, where he can be stalked as:

Twitter: **@KevlinHenney**
Medium: **@kevlinhenney**
Instagram: **@kevlin.henney**

Maria Herring

Maria was born in the UK but has spent the last decade travelling around the world teaching the English language. This nomadic lifestyle, which sometimes resulted in tragic distances from bookshops, was when she discovered the joys of writing. Her first novel, *Legacy of Warrior Queen*, was published while she was abroad. She returned to the UK for a bit to work on her first Science Fiction novel and was mentored by Philip K Dick Award nominee Liz Williams. She's back in France, and the first two books in her new fantasy series, *The Healing Glass* (Age of Academicians 1) and *Awakening Mages* (Age of Academicians 2) are available now.

When Maria isn't writing she's pen and ink drawing, a new-found passion, which she hopes she'll be able to incorporate in her future books. She may be a full-grown adult, but she still likes books with pictures.

Feel free to check out her verbal and visual doodles at: **www.mariaherring.com**

Barry Hollow

Barry lives in Bristol but was born and raised in Ayrshire and although his poetry covers many themes, it often features a sprinkling of Old Scots. His debut collection – *Viaducts and River Views* – is due for release in 2021 by A.B. Baird Publishing and he has a pamphlet length collection within – *Symphonies of the Wild-Hearted* – from the same publisher. He will also have a chapter in the upcoming anthology – *Healing* – by Magesoul Publishing.

Barry has been featured regularly on BBC Radio and is emerging on the spoken word scene in Bristol.

You can find him on:

Instagram:
@thehollowgram

Twitter:
@barryhollow

Scott Lewis

Scott Lewis trained as a journalist, and spent time with the Sunderland Echo, BBC Somerset and as a freelancer in China before switching his attention to PR and marketing. He took up fiction writing in late 2012, and in 2013 he won the Bristol Festival of Literature Short Story Competition. His work has appeared in several publications including *Airship Shape and Bristol Fashion, The Kraken Rises!, The First Line Literary Journal,* numerous anthologies and several short story compilations.

When not putting pen to paper Scott is an avid board and wargamer, roleplayer, and amateur photographer. He enjoys hiking, outdoor pursuits and gallavanting all over the country doing silly things.

He lives in Bristol with his partner and their Evil Feline Overlord, and can occasionally be found on:

Twitter: **@GntlmnRogue**

Kevin MacCabe

Kevin MacCabe is a Dublin born writer whose work weaves environmental issues into multiple genres. He has previously written sitcom scripts and has a short story collection of climate change fables. He is currently submitting his first novel, an allegorical climate change tale.

He has flash fiction published at @Reflexfiction and @FlashFicMag and his story *We Are Where We Are* was first published in Dark Mountain's *Fire* Edition.

You can find him online: **@6040split**

Alex Nicholas

Alex Nicholas has always been a daydreamer. As a child, he didn't make the rounders team because he was absently picking daisies instead of trying to catch the ball. Now he sometimes turns those daydreams into stories, with a novel or two sitting in a drawer marked "please finish me".

In his other plotline, he works for the NHS as an MRI radiographer.

He can be found on Twitter: **@AlexNicholas82**

Kimberly Nugent

Kimberly Nugent lives in the American Southwest with her family and two cats. In her 'day job', she edits and develops tabletop RPGs with Red Scar Publishing and others.

Kimberly revisited poetry writing 3 years ago, after falling in love with speculative poetry, and you can find her pieces with *Star*Line*, *Scifaikuest*, and other publications. She has been nominated for a Dwarf Star award for poetry published in 2018 and 2019.

You can find her on Twitter: **@BlueTeaEditing**

M. E. Rodman

M.E Rodman writes LGBT+ fantasy with a dark edge and occasional stories of horror and the uncanny.

Their short fiction has appeared in *Airship Shape and Bristol Fashion, The Dark Half of the Year, Goddesses of the Sea* and *A Picture's Worth,* and online at *Expanded Horizons* and *Zetetic, a Record of Unusual Inquiry.* A short story *The Selkie; A Tale of Love, Obsession and the Sea,* was adapted and performed as a live radio play for the *Sanctum Project* in 2015.

Their debut novel, *Blood and Thorn*, was released in January 2020, from Kristell Ink Publishing.

They have an MA in Creative Writing from Edinburgh Napier and are a current guest editor for Fantasia Divinity Publishing. They live near Glasgow, with their partner, child, a small dog, and a large cat.

Social media contacts:

Website: **me-rodman.wixsite.com/writer**
Facebook: **/merodmanwriter**
Twitter: **@thecantingbones**

Ken Shinn

Ken Shinn may not be the God of Hell-Fire, but he'll beg you to burn with his tale for this anthology.

Now 56 years old and currently resident in Trowbridge with his two marvellous cats, as well as this book, more tales from him can be found in the recently-published *The Third BHF Book Of Horror Stories* and *The Unofficial Doctor Who Annual, 1989*. He's also due to appear soon in Theresa Derwin's *Flashes Of Hope* collection, and still aims to get his first novel, *Case Of The Vapours*, published within his current lifetime somehow.

Now, where did he put that Scorpion Pepper sauce? There's a chilli to be made…

Amanda Staples

Amanda Staples is fascinated by the workings of the mind and has a minor obsession with death. This led her to become a hypnotherapist in lieu of an undertaker.

Her writing is fuelled by pots of tea and drams of whisky. Her work has featured in anthologies and various literary magazines and has been recorded for podcasts and youtube. She self-published a recipe book and is currently indulging her novel writing ambition.

Her play *Weston on a Sunday* has been staged in Croydon and Bristol.

She has read at Bath Lit Fringe Fest, Bristol Lit Fest, Talking Tales and Writers Unchained events in Bristol, and Stroud Short Stories.

You can follow her online:

Facebook: **/scribestaples**
Twitter: **@scribestaples1**

Pete W. Sutton

Pete W. Sutton is a writer and editor. His first book – *A Tiding of Magpies* – was shortlisted for the British Fantasy Awards in 2017 for Best Collection. His last novel – *Seven Deadly Swords* – was published by Grimbold Books and is available to order from all good bookshops. He has edited a number of short story anthologies, the latest – *Forgotten Sidekicks* – was published in April 2020.

You can find out more about Pete at his website: **petewsutton.com**

or find him posting on Twitter: **@suttope**